A Secret In Onyx

Jessica Florence

This is a work of fiction. Names, places, characters, and events are fictitious in every regard. Any similarities to actual events, and persons, living or dead, are purely coincidental. Any trademarks, service marks, product names, or named features are assumed to be the property of their respective owners and are used only for reference. There is no implied endorsement if any of those terms are used. Except for review purposes, the reproduction of this book in whole or part, electronically or mechanically, constitutes a copyright violation.

Jessica Florence© **2020**

Editing by Magnifico Manuscripts

Proofreading by Virginia Tesi Carey

Cover by Opulent Swag and Design

This Book is Dedicated to

Karen, Lorraine, Becca, Rochelle, and Casey.

Thank you for giving me a real chance.

Chapter One

They say when mankind fell, a black flash streaked across the sky. People died where they stood. Planes and cars stopped instantly. The world went dark in mere seconds. I wished I could remember what it looked like to see planes in the sky or cars moving along the roads instead of husks of the great machines scattered across the land. Sometimes in the quiet of the night when the darkness covered me like a security blanket, I dreamed of what life was like before it all ended.

Tor, my boyfriend and traveling companion, liked to hold me close against his hard chest and recall what he remembered. He was older than me. As far as I knew, I was twenty-three years old and he was twenty-eight. The day life changed, I had been three and alone. A neighbor, Mariam, took care of me until she died six months ago. Tor wasn't a psychopath like others I had encountered on the roads, so sticking together was the best decision for both of us.

"What were you thinking just now?" He peered at me with his chestnut brown hair brushing against his matching lashes. Rundown, he desperately needed a trim. His arm tightened around me, making me feel warm and safe. Most of the time, I didn't feel safe in this dangerous world. There were days when I thought it wasn't worth the fight to survive this hell. Maybe I would just slit my own throat or let the Dramens take me and eat me. But every time I had that thought, Tor was there, as if he noticed me falling down and out of his reach.

"I was thinking about the 'before.'" I dreamed wistfully of the past often and how different it would have been if nothing had changed.

"Of course, you were." I didn't have to look at his face to know he smiled lovingly at me, finding enjoyment in my dreams of the past.

"Continue the story, please. I won't nod off, I promise." Ever since I had met Tor, near the small community of normal survivors in what used to be called North Carolina, he'd told me tales to keep my mind busy and give me hope. Hope to keep me from the darkness that beckoned me to join the rest of humanity.

"Anything for you."

I knew in my soul he would always be there for me, in whatever way I needed, except the one way I wished to be joined with him as a couple. He always kept me at a distance instead of touching me like I knew he wanted to act upon.

"I forget where I was in the story. Had Queen Olyndria married King Lachan from the kingdom across the land yet?"

I nodded against his chest, my hands idly drawing swirls across his dirt-covered green shirt, which was soft despite the grit. "She just gave birth to the princess."

I closed my eyes, forgetting about the "before" as he continued with the story of the magical Fae, fantastical tales of royal queens, kings, daring princesses, handsome princes, dragons, and cores made of nature inside them. They were stories from a fairy tale book, but I loved hearing them just as much as I obsessed hearing about life when things were simpler.

Tor began the story. "Queen Olyndria was a beautiful Fae with brown hair and pale skin that shimmered like a jewel. The royal Fae had gem cores, signaling their power. They lived among the world of men in a hidden realm where they helped protect us from the evil creatures who lived there. Most stayed in a particular part of the realm with their king, an awful man named King Verin. The queen finally wed a king from another land, and they had a baby, Princess Nyx. She had lavender hair and pale skin like her mother and eyes of the deepest royal purple from the amethyst core inside her."

I sighed. Such a difference from my light brown skin, messy hair with curls of brown, and almond-shaped eyes that Tor said reminded him of a forest in spring—a bright green mixed with yellow and brown flakes around my irises. However, I had come to terms with myself, even if I wasn't a gorgeous Fae.

Tor never mentioned what the princess's powers were, but he said she was promised to be the most powerful of them all. "I bet she met a prince and they had a large wedding full of dancing," I muttered wistfully. People didn't have parties or large weddings anymore. If you managed to not be taken by the Dramens and made into a wife, either willing or not, then you spent life in a safe community or on the road, hiding.

"I don't think they did, actually. The Fae legends say King Verin released a darkness into the realm that took away their powers, making them defenseless to his takeover of their world. The princess would save them all, so her parents encased her in an onyx tomb. The queen used the last of her powers to save her daughter and it drove her mad. Not a very happy ending to this story." His voice became solemn, and remorse gutted me for requesting he tell me this tale.

"Well, I'm gonna choose to believe the story is real, and eventually the princess will be released from the onyx and will save everyone, maybe even us poor humans."

Part of me knew he made this story up to keep me distracted from the evil around us. The other part of me believed his story came from some truth. Somewhere out there, the Fae existed.

I fell asleep, thinking of a purple-haired woman encased in onyx who would one day rise and save the world.

Chapter Two

The sun came up early this time of year, which used to be called autumn. We'd made camp in a rundown church, and while I appreciated the rays of light beaming through the torn curtains, I wished they would have let me sleep longer in darkness. Vines covered the ceiling with spider webs hanging between the leaves. The pews were strewn haphazardly, like a monster had come into this place of worship and destroyed it. Dirt, grass, and twenty-year-old bibles were scattered across the tile floor. The hard ground scratched the exposed skin from the holes in my clothes.

It wasn't wise to stay in one place for long when you were in a small group. Dramens had daily search raids to find survivors and take them back to their keep. There were four sections of the country that used to be called the United States. First, the Northwest side, where the people became more like the great beasts that roamed the lands. I had heard they would capture you and you'd be forced to either join them or die. The Southwest Dramens had camps everywhere. Their hearth fires looked like stars that had fallen and scattered across the deserts. They, along with the Northeast ones, were the expert hunters. They liked to chase after survivors, then sell them to the highest bidder. Paper money became useless after everything happened. Dramens preferred to be paid in nickel, silver, gold, and iron coins. Gold used to be the top of the currency pyramid, but not anymore. Iron reigned as king in these lands. The more iron you had, the richer you were. The Southeast Dramens, the most hateful of beings, liked to eat their prey, human and animal alike. They raped, pillaged, and took pleasure as they saw fit. These had broken into the colony where I had grown up.

My heart beat rapidly, my breaths stuck in my throat, and my belly twisted. Their horrible faces would forever be burned into my memory—blonde, long hair, beards coated in blood, and yellow-crusted teeth dripping with the remnants of whatever throats they'd ripped out moments before.

I sat up abruptly, looking around. I saw the green in the trees, the sun shining, and the man still sleeping next to me. I had to remember this reality existed and the memory, as horrible as it was, was just an awful memory.

In the middle of the land, where the corners of the territories connected, the Dramen's capital rested, a place we'd managed to skate by undetected a few weeks ago. The leaders of the lands lived in a palace of stone and iron at its center. Their king and queen sat upon thrones of human bones and skulls in the great halls. They rose to power two years after the fall of mankind. We humans had been in such chaos that many didn't know how to survive. Such disarray let the weak be easily preyed upon by the vicious without much fight. Dramens were the elite now, and everyone else lived until they were either converted or killed.

My labored breaths slowed and my chest didn't ache as much. The sweat covering my body had cooled in the early morning breeze. Tor sleepily stretched beside me on the old mat beneath him. What I wouldn't give to lay on a real bed, soft, warm, and clean. Clean. I'd been wearing the same cargo pants and long-sleeve shirt for weeks. We really needed to go into a small town soon for supplies.

"Sleep well?" His husky voice was cute, as well as the smile growing on those perfect bow-shaped lips. I never stood a chance resisting Tor's charms, so when I lowered my head to press a gentle kiss to the creator of the warm feelings stirring in my belly, it wasn't of my own doing.

"Not really, but it's time to get up." I tried to be honest, even if people didn't like what I had to say. Mariam wanted me to soften my words, but that conversation usually had her muttering about how much of a wild girl I had become. After surviving the apocalypse, I needed to stay true to myself since the breaths I had were a gift. I wouldn't waste words by telling lies.

"Nightmares?" Tor's calloused hand caressed the side of my cheek, gently pushing my wild brown hair back behind my ear. He always demonstrated care with me. I liked it, considering the alternative, but I wished he didn't treat me like I'd break. I could sort of hunt and fight. Mariam made sure I learned the different skills I could in the community we'd lived in. I found some things came easier than others. Thankfully I was a fair cook.

He stared at me with his deep blue eyes, knowing I was plagued with nightmares. "Yeah, I'm OK, though. Really. Now let's go check those traps, unless you want to do something else instead." I waggled my eyebrows suggestively. My fingers grazed the skin over his hard cheek bones, down his closely shaved beard, and to his bobbing throat.

"I am pretty hungry." His sleepy tone he had moments ago did not sound so tired anymore. I knew he meant hungry for actual food and not me. Never me. Having that knowledge didn't stop me from being a brat to test his willpower.

"Hm, me, too." My driven fingers moved down his lean torso, admiring the body he'd conditioned in order to survive. His nostrils flared, and his dark blue eyes turned ravenous. *Could it be? Did I finally push Tor over the edge after months of this indisputable tension?* My breath stilled in my chest as I waited for him to make a move. It became tiring, sometimes, constantly being the one to initiate contact between us. I needed to know he wanted me.

"Let's go check the traps." He blew out his own breath like he'd been holding it in. The disappointment showed on my face. Tor stretched, drawing my gaze to his lean body.

"I'll explain everything one day. All of this will make sense, and I swear I will bed you the way you deserve. I swear, Sapphira." His hand cupped my cheek as he leaned in to kiss my lips, his body tense like he could lose control and snap me at any moment.

"OK."

He said there were things he couldn't tell me until we reached a community in a place that used to be called California. Supposedly, it was the last and largest location of survivors on the continent, a town where even the Dramens couldn't touch them. I longed for that freedom from fear where children laughed and people grew old together and made friends.

It was probably a fool's dreams, one that would turn out to be nothing in the end. Tor and I had passed many towns that had once been great cities. Beautiful scenes had survived after the world ended. Mankind was coming to an end, and all that remained were husks of a past life.

Tor, satisfied with my answer for now, grabbed his quiver of arrows and compound bow. With a huff, he jumped out an old broken window of the church to check the perimeter. He would always be my guard and protector first, and boyfriend second.

Most of the time I loved his protective side. I would always be OK with him. However, there were times when I craved a lover and passion, the type of love Mariam used to read to me in books, a feeling that made you willing to cross oceans and move mountains. I didn't know how to express that kind of love in words or even thoughts. It was inside me, like it had existed once before, and then disappeared. The words were lost, and until I found what my deepest desires looked for, it had no name in my heart, just a feeling, an unyielding desire.

Chapter Three

We didn't catch anything, which usually signified trouble for us.

Ever since the majority of humans had died, animal life had flourished. Catching nothing meant something else lingered nearby and had hunted the creatures, most likely Dramens.

Tor and I moved west as quickly as we could, avoiding any unfriendly people as we traveled. Thankfully, my body had gotten used to small rations of food and water. The muscles I had were puny from lack of good nutrition, but I could run quickly and quietly. Swiftness was a gift, Mariam had said, one that had saved my life a few times already. Tor ran fast as well, always light on his feet without any sound. We moved like we'd been created from the woods themselves, landing on the balls of our feet without crinkling leaves beneath our boots.

"We only have one more day until we reach the tree and the colony." Tor slowed to a full stop. We hadn't heard anything for hours, but Dramens were stealthy, so they could hunt and not be hunted.

"Good! What I wouldn't do for some hot food and a bath." My body vitally needed sustenance. We only had a few pieces of dried deer left in Tor's pack, which wasn't enough to survive on for much longer.

"Priorities," Tor laughed, a sound I loved to hear and heard often. He was a bright light in this dark world, smiles and hope bundled in an attractive package.

"Admit it, you would love a bath, too. You stink! We both stink!"

"Well, now that you mention it, sleeping next to you does make my eyes water most nights." Tor always made jokes, making the most out of any situation. I rolled my eyes, shaking my head in exasperation.

A stick cracking echoed to our right. Our heads turned instantly. The Dramens had found us. The hairs on my arms rose, and my heartbeat thumped in my chest so loudly I feared our intruder would hear it. *This was it.* My hand reached for Tor's muscular fingers, needing to feel him, to remember we were in this together.

Tor's eyes narrowed on the location of the stick breaking, his other hand reaching for his bow slowly. With my free hand, I grabbed the sword from the belt at my hip. We would fight and probably die, but we would not go easily for these beasts of men.

I looked at Tor, memorizing his features.

"This is not our end," he whispered as he gazed at me. I nodded, trusting him, although my nerves did not surrender to that trust so easily. We readied ourselves for an attack, eyes turning toward the woods with the determination to fight.

A deer leaped into view from a large tree in the direction of the sound we'd heard. A deer, not a Dramen.

Tor let go of my hand instantly and had an arrow docked against the bow. In mere seconds, the deer lay dead on the ground. Tor never missed a shot.

At least I would have some food tonight to comfort the unease that had settled inside my belly from the thoughts of our impending death.

I wasn't scared of dying. However, that didn't mean I wanted to be tortured, sold as a slave, or used for other nefarious purposes like breeding.

"I still don't trust these woods. Let's take it somewhere safe," Tor murmured softly, his gaze darting around the trees cautiously. There could still be something out there, and his instincts were always right.

"I'll go look for somewhere safe. You do the deer," I told him, as I searched the woods. He wanted to fling a retort at me. Tor was sweet, kind, and brave. He was everything I loved. He wanted to be my protector; he wanted to do everything for me so that I wouldn't have a chance of being in danger. Sweet. However, I was no damsel in distress.

He wanted to tell me no, but he also knew this was a fight he wouldn't win so he remained silent. Though his posture remained rigid, his jaw ticked while he clenched back his argument.

"Stay safe. If you need help, scream loud enough to shake the trees." I'd have to snuggle up close to him tonight after this. I nodded, pleading with my eyes for him to understand that I needed this. This freedom. The world sucked. I couldn't be some princess locked away while he took care of everything for me. He knew it, too. I left to find us shelter so we could make jerky, and it went against everything inside him to let me go. He didn't come after me; he showed trust, and I smiled.

I made no sound with every step I took, my boots never crunched on a dead leaf, and my hand always stayed attached to my sword. This land around looked different than I was used to, more rugged and dry. The mountains near us were not like the rolling hills of the East. Trees thinned and there wouldn't be much cover for us soon. After we'd made our food tonight, we needed to get somewhere else quick. Being out in the open made us vulnerable.

Sweat dropped from my brow when I found an old shack hidden near a creek. Dust coated the old and rundown wood. It looked like it might fall down with a gentle breeze. My gut told me it was safe, except a creeping suspicion in my mind wouldn't let me drop my guard. I scoped out the area around it, checking nearby for Dramens who could be waiting for someone to fall for their shack trap. I found none, just an old hunting shack someone had used before, though not recently, if all the bugs and rot were any evidence. It was the only thing I'd found in the vicinity and would have to do.

A three-legged chair, a dirty rug, and an axe resting in the corner were the lone inhabitants of this small temporary home. Well, the bugs were present, too. I didn't care for bugs, but we lacked options.

I heard noise outside the window . . . not feet stepping, only a manly grunt. I ducked down and peered with just my eyes showing through the broken window. Tor steadily carried the deer over his shoulder about half a mile away, having followed me with tracking tricks he'd never shown me, even though I begged to know. I wouldn't hear his grunts from here unless he made loud noises, which would not be typical Tor behavior.

My stomach clenched at the only possible conclusion. Someone else was here.

Chapter Four

I had no time to brace myself from the splintering wood exploding in front of me. A large man with dark hair, tan skin, and leather clothes burst through the door. His face had black paint on it and feathers covered his shoulders. A Dramen was here to capture his prey.

His rough, callused hands gripped my arm, then my hair. I didn't scream for fear there were more and they would follow the sounds. He did not care that it hurt or if I was broken before he used me and took me to sell on the market.

I was no one's slave.

My fingers gripped the hilt of my sword, ready to fight, to survive. He grabbed the belt it was on and ripped it from my hip. The pinch of the leather breaking against my skin added to the consuming pain of him dragging me away from the shack by my hair.

I had to do something. Tor would see me and come, but if they had a horse then that would be it for me.

My teeth clenched from the barely contained rage as I twisted myself against his hold. I didn't care if I wound up with bald patches in my hair. My hand reached for his manhood and twisted hard. He yelled, and if any of his friends were near, they would be on their way to his aid soon. His grip relaxed and I kicked his broad body away from me. Tears flooded my eyes from the yank on my head. I scrambled for the shack and the dusty axe I'd seen. My sword had fallen behind the Dramen and would be too much of a risk to scramble for and potentially fail.

As soon as my fingers wrapped around the handle, arms of a feral man gripped my legs. My face fell forward to the wall. Intense pain bloomed in my nose, followed by the cascading warmth of blood flowing down my face, soaking my dirty shirt.

The hatred in his narrowed glare told me there would be no mercy. The anger from my little twist would override his will to keep me alive. Dramens had lost their humanity and mercy. All that remained was anarchy.

He leaned closer. The scent of dirt and sweat assaulted my damaged nose, giving me the urge to vomit.

A wet tongue flicked against my bloody chin, as I cried out in disgust. His breath made my stomach churn, and his rough touch roamed over my torso. He was playing with his food before he killed it.

Not today, asshole.

The axe in my hand moved up . . . up . . . past my head and into his wide-eyed face.

The dull blade did its job. The Dramen crumbled to the ground, his heavy weight shaking the shack as he fell. An arrow protruding from his back caught my attention. Tor had arrived. Steady hands cradled my bloody face instantly.

"You're OK?" he growled, his voice low enough to be a whisper in the open forest. His rage was palpable in the air around us.

"I'm fine. We need to move." The sound of wet, ripping skin and the scraping of metal against bone echoed in the small shack as I pulled the axe out of the Dramen's face.

Tor retrieved his arrow and cut as much meat of the deer we could place in a plastic bag. My sword belt was torn, so I did my best to tie it around my waist until I could find another. We were gone in fifteen minutes. The majority of the deer was left for wild scavengers to eat. More Dramens would be coming and if we didn't haul ass, we would be dead.

My face ached, and my muscles burned like they were on fire as we moved quickly across the barren land. The desert turned cold as the dark approached. We needed sleep. Tor had been quiet since we left the shack by the creek. It was a lethal calm that had me glancing his way, watching him nervously.

Was he afraid I could have died? Was he feeling anger for not being there? For letting me go off by myself?

When we'd stop, I'd ask him.

Hours into the night, we finally found a small abandoned town. The Dramens of these regions preferred the outdoors to towns. Their nature was wild, and houses were too confining. For once we were safer here than hiding in the trees or brush.

Walking through an abandoned town was unlike anything else imaginable. People had died here, not just from Dramens but from the day mankind fell. They had people who loved them, jobs and lives to live. Then one day it all disappeared. Coffee mugs still sat next to papers on the breakfast table, and cars were parked in the middle of the road where people had sat in traffic. Stop signs that people held for children to cross the road safely lay on the cracked asphalt, weeds growing over the once heavily walked paths.

"Which house, dear?" I politely asked Tor, hoping the fluttering of my eyelashes and sweet voice would turn the hard line of his lips into a smile. It didn't. He silently picked a house in the middle of the small town. It had many places to hide, escape routes, and a quick run to the woods if needed. Ten miles away, a much larger city dwelled, so this was perfect, away from the desert lands where the Dramens camped and the city where they liked to hide and capture people who went looking for supplies.

"Places like this always give me the creeps," I whispered as we walked through the dry overgrown grass and opened the metal gate to the stone house.

"Never gets easier," he mumbled, as the door opened without hesitation. I guess we should be thankful it wasn't locked, and my mind unfortunately wondered as to why it remained in that state. Maybe the person was out walking his pet when he died, leaving the door unlocked. Or maybe they survived the apocalypse and deserted it, not caring if their house was secure.

The dry, stale air in the house smelled like mold. Home sweet home.

"We need to clean that face of yours," he announced, then looked around the house for anyone hiding who may attack us. He searched for medical supplies. The blood had long since dried on my face, making me crave a bath even more.

The sheer curtains of the dark living room were drawn and thankfully, I could see everything. Framed pictures of a happy family hung on the walls. Little knickknacks were strewn above a fireplace mantel that must have held value to the family who lived here. I hated being here, like we were intruding on this family. Or if I was being more honest with myself, their tomb.

"Sapphira!" Tor hollered and I quickly moved toward the direction of his voice. Tor stood in a small pink bathroom with a bottle of water in his hand and a fluffy pink towel in the other.

"They didn't really have much that we could use, but at least we can clean the blood up. I might need to reset the nose, too." He winced. He would hate to inflict additional pain on me. Once again, we had to do what we had to do.

"Just do it." My fingers gripped the door jam, and I clenched my teeth. I wanted to be done with today, eat something, and sleep.

It hurt like hell as Tor moved my nose back into place, cleaned the blood, and toweled it dry. He didn't try to soothe me or talk about what happened earlier. He left me alone in the bathroom before I could broach the subject. I looked at the woman in the old dusty mirror, hoping I'd see some badass, instead of the rundown, dirty, crazy-haired one.

"You killed a Dramen today, Sapphira. You can talk to him." I gave myself a pep talk before finding Tor outside making a fire to cook the deer meat.

Chapter Five

"I think we need to talk about today." I sat next to him. This house had what I bet was a nice backyard in its prime. The pool was an algae and bug-infested pond, with vines reaching the edge from the wall surrounding the premises. A perfect setting to keep our fire hidden and to cook the small amount of deer meat we had.

"I don't think I can yet."

"Then you can listen."

"Besides a broken nose and a sore scalp, I am OK. I fell for a trap, one I should have seen. We made it out alive; we're OK. Please don't let this come between us. Don't let this stop you from letting me do things on my own." My stomach churned, waiting for his retort. We didn't argue much since we met, and I didn't know what I'd do without him if he decided to leave.

His head dropped, and his tan hands reached up to rub his face in frustration.

"I just—" I searched for the words to ease his worry, his broken voice interrupting my thoughts.

"I can't lose you."

I hated seeing this kind of sadness in him. My hand brushed back the hairs covering his face.

"You won't lose me. It's me and you, Tor." Warmth blossomed in my belly as I looked at him in this moment. He loved me; I knew it. With him by my side, I felt cherished and safe.

"I love you, Tor." My lips pressed against his shoulder, showing him my feelings with my gentle touch.

I met his tear-brimmed stare with my watered eyes. Our lips met in a fury of desperation and fear for this life we had. We couldn't lose us in this moment . . . this love, this closeness between each other.

"I love you, Sapphira."

I laid back against the hard ground and brought Tor's body with me. He went with no hesitation this time. We kissed under the vibrant star-covered sky, living for the now in each other's arms. Despite his warm body on top of mine, and the hot kisses against my skin and lips, the chilled air nipped at my bones.

"Let's go inside and get some sleep." Tor leaned back, kissing my cheeks before slowly crawling off of me. His hands stretched out for mine to take, and in one swift move, as if I weighed nothing, I stood on my feet.

We didn't go any further than explorative touches and lips on exposed skin. There was something more between us since we'd uttered those sweet words of love. We'd make it to the safe haven and then there would be time to finally be with each other, without worries of starvation or the Dramens attacking us. We could date and court each other, and he wouldn't have to worry about me.

We fell asleep in each other's arms on someone else's bed. I tried not to think about the pictures of a smiling woman and man staring at me from the nightstand.

Time was precious and I wasn't going to waste any more of it thinking about the past. I had to think about the future, and what my role would be in it.

**

The clothes in the closet were old and had a stale-air scent clinging to them. They were cleaner and had no holes, which was better than the clothes I currently wore.

I decided on a pale green shirt and black yoga pants. I kept my boots and found a leather belt to work as my sword holster. Tor came back from the bathroom dressed in new clothes as well—loose-fitting denim jeans and a blue cotton shirt.

"Only half a day until we get to the red tree. That's where the community is. Just past the large green sign that says Yosemite National Park." Tor spoke aloud, mostly for himself than for me. I knew the way there; we'd looked at it on a map so many times I had the route memorized.

An electrical sensation buzzed in my veins from the excitement of freedom. No more on the run, no more Dramens, no more of this life I'd lived. I was ready for something new, something different.

"Let's eat some deer and get out of here. I'm ready to get there and rest for days." I grinned thinking about the lazing around without the threat of danger. My muscles and feet could use a little downtime. Since we'd traveled on foot across the continent, my poor body was tired down to the bones.

There was still time for a kiss before we left, so I tackled a newly dressed Tor to the bed and smothered his face with dramatic kisses, loud smooch sounds echoing around the room. It wasn't often we got to laugh and smile in our environment. I wanted to steal a little bit of time for fun.

"When we get to where we're going, you're gonna be in for it." He rolled me over on the bed, his body looming over mine. I prayed, wished, and hoped he meant what I wanted him to mean.

"You're going to punish me for being so bad," I teased, pulling my bottom lip between my teeth.

"We'll just have to make it there and see." He leaned down, his blue eyes on me as he pressed one kiss upon my grinning lips.

Then as quickly as it began, our moment was over. Reality clinched our thoughts and reminded us that we needed to eat and move out with haste. The longer we stayed here, the more likely someone would come scouting and we'd be found. We double-checked our inventory, water, food, and weapons. It would have to do in our final hours to the hopefully blessed destination.

After our food had settled in our stomachs, we hit the grass-covered road. Over our journey, I attempted to overlook the bones we saw. In the woods, there weren't many to see, since most people weren't out in the wild when everything happened. In towns like this, it was hard to ignore. The drier climates without the humidity preserved them slightly more than the other side of the continent.

There wasn't anything I could do about it now. The more I saw, the more I wanted to know their story, to bury them, and pray to the heavens that they found peace after dying.

"Keep moving forward," Tor whispered as we passed a school bus crashed into a light pole. It had dried vines growing over it. A heavy feeling settled over me; my hands trembled at the sight. I knew not all of the kids on the bus had died that day. I also knew there were now bones left in the faded yellow tomb.

"Nothing I can do," I whispered to myself and closed my eyes. I couldn't change the past; I could only move forward.

We left the town and followed a back road that would skirt around the larger city and lead us to our new home.

Two hours passed, and I thought about how much I hoped our destination truly existed, and it wasn't overrun, destroyed, or a lie. I didn't know if I would be able to muster up hope if it weren't true. Once someone lost hope, he or she lost everything. Hope pushed you, drove you to greatness . . . the lack of it would destroy you. I decided to let go of the worries and simply hope. We would make it, it would be there, and we would be OK.

"Hello, travelers."

All hope I had crashed and burned like the planes falling out of the sky on the end of days. A group of three Dramens stood before us, armed with an axe, a bow, and a gun.

Chapter Six

My body froze in place; every muscle locked. I didn't know what to do. We were outnumbered, and while we could fight, we couldn't take all three of them.

They looked similar in size, maybe six feet, and tough. Cords of muscles bulged out from their leather and feather-covered attire. Signature black paint smudged their face and arms. They had weapons strapped to every part of their body.

What scared me the most was their eyes—the menace and the feral look in them that promised such awful things.

"I like the girl. Can we keep her, Dak?" the one on the left said to one of the others without taking his eyes off me.

"Nah. We'll sell them both. I bet they'd pay a pretty penny for these two at the Iron Castle." The man in the middle smiled, his yellow-stained teeth making me cringe even more.

"Sorry, gentlemen, we are already traveling somewhere else. You won't be taking us." Tor stood tall. His dominant hand twitched, ready to reach for his weapon, all the while keeping his eyes on the man in the middle named Dak. The leader, the Dramen who held the gun in his hands, aimed at our heads.

Guns were not something you saw often. They hoarded them in the Iron Castle with the king and queen, which meant the fools had found the weapons.

"Don't think you can stop us. Let's go peacefully to camp, then we will head to the city," Dak said with the confidence of someone knowing he had the upper hand. I looked at Tor, just as he turned his gaze to me. We were going to fight; I didn't think we'd win but we were going for it anyway. I sure as shit would rather die than be taken to the Iron City.

Faster than I'd seen him move before, Tor had his knife in hand and threw it at Dak's shoulder. It hit, and it hit hard. His body fell backward, and a gunshot echoed around the woods as he landed on the ground. He had the instinct to pull the trigger, but the bullet missed.

The other two shot forward with weapons ready to kill. Tor took the one on the left, the one that wanted to keep me, and I found the one on the right with the axe. I knew how to fight. I could do this.

He swung hard, the sound of the metal slicing through the air buzzing in my ears. I kicked when he tried to right himself again, knocking him in the side, his feet staggering from the loss of balance. This time he swung up, to impale the blade in my throat. I moved quickly, dancing as if I was a warrior on a stage instead of the nutritionally deprived girl moving for her life.

My fingers gripped my sword and I arced it low. The wet sound of skin being sliced filling the air. His groan echoed against the trees before he dropped to his knees to press his dirty hands to his wound.

I looked over to my love and watched as time seemed to slow. Tor's head was between a Dramen's arms and the sight made my knees wobble. My stomach dropped to my feet and my throat ached from the tears brewing. The Dramen would kill Tor. My Tor.

I reacted. My feet were no longer frozen to the desert ground. I moved with an instinct to protect, and before I could blink, the Dramen's head rolled on the ground. Blood dripped from the tip of my sword to the dirt.

Tor's eyes were wide at what I'd done.

We ran and the booming sounds of gunshots rang around us. Dak fired at our moving forms, or maybe he was signaling for help. Either way, we needed to run faster than the dry wind that moved against our rustling clothes. Faster and faster, until my lungs wouldn't expand beyond a short intake of dry breath.

"I need water," I coughed out, the dryness in my mouth and throat making it hard to speak. I needed a break. Tor handed me the water and kept an eye on the surroundings. The three Dramens were behind us, one dead, two wounded, except I knew there were more out there. Mass numbers of vile humans hunting their prey, waiting.

For a moment like this.

Tor had an arrow in his leg before I could scream. They were coming from every direction.

"Sapphira. You run. You run there and don't look back. I will meet you there. I will find you again, I swear it."

I shook my head back and forth, again and again. I wouldn't leave him. We could fight.

"Sapphira, I will see you again." He gripped behind my neck and kissed me hard, a promise seeping into my soul. This was not our end.

I didn't want to run and leave him. Tears rolled past my brown lashes, spilling down my cheeks, as the anguish of the choice inside me formed.

"We could fight," I whispered as eight Dramens surrounded us, closing in slowly, tauntingly. They knew their prey had nowhere to go and wanted to play with our minds.

"No, you will run, and you won't stop. Listen to me, Sapphira. You fucking run as soon as I give you the opening. I will see you again. I love you." His forehead rested against mine, our eyes closed, giving ourselves this last moment before all hell broke loose.

"I love you. I'll see you," I whispered and kissed him softly, his lips wet from my tears flowing onto his skin. Our final act of love tasted of salty tears, with scents of bloody dirt and a promise to survive.

It happened quick. Tor wouldn't give them a chance to take me. His arrow docked on his bow and released to my left. The Dramen went down and I ran. The opening was just enough for me to squeeze through. I heard yelling for someone to get me, and I heard a bellow of pain echo across the barren lands. Tor.

I wanted to go back. I wanted to dig my heels into the dirt and turn around. He was in pain. They were hurting him, and they would hurt me. My painful memories showed exactly what they would do if they captured me.

I told him I'd go; I'd find the community. Maybe he'd find a way to meet me there, or maybe I could gather an army and get him.

Maybe. Maybe. Maybe.

There was no stopping. The wind dried the tears on my cheeks as I ran.

I would see Tor again, even if I had to march on the Iron City myself to get him.

Chapter Seven

    I moved until I couldn't muster one more step. Every muscle in my body ached, but my heart hurt the most. I still had much ground to cover before I reached the tree Tor drilled into my brain for memory. So many more burdened steps to make. Every inch toward the community took me farther away from Tor. I wanted to stop, but I wouldn't tarnish what he did. He gave me time to escape a horrifying fate that I wouldn't endure again.

    The day had turned into night. The lands had changed from desert to lush, large trees, and mountains with white tips. It even looked like rain was coming, if the drop in temperature and dark clouds were an indication. With every step, I came closer to the safe haven . . . so close, but I couldn't go on right now. I needed to rest. I had to gather what small strength I had left in my body to finish this.

    I found a large tree and collapsed against its bulging roots. Tor had the water and the food, so I had no sustenance. I'd have to look for something soon to replenish the pain gnawing in my belly and throat. However, everything could wait for a few minutes.

    My fingers dug against the muscles of my thighs. Soreness blossomed with every touch. The massage would help move the pain out until I stopped again. I stretched to my toes, opening up every vein in my body that pumped blood faster to soothe my erratically beating heart.

"Only a few more minutes," I told myself sternly. I couldn't stay here much longer than twenty minutes. There was still a possibility of Dramens nearby, and I would likely be passed out and not wake up for hours if I stayed. I felt tired . . . so tired.

Using the tree to steady my shaky legs, I stood, wobbling from side to side to get my center of gravity under control. I took one step, then another, then another.

I focused on every stride, my only goal to keep moving. It didn't matter how fast, just that I didn't stop. A small creek surrounded by a group of trees and large gray rocks appeared ahead. I heard the water streaming along the bank, making my mouth feel unnaturally dry. My knees crashed to the ground as soon as I made it to the edge, and my hands scooped up water as fast as I could summon the movement. The fresh liquid must have come down from the mountains around me. Once the threat of passing out from dehydration ebbed, I rose to my feet again and continued. I'd already passed the big green, debilitated sign a while ago.

I scanned for any sign of a safe haven nearby. Walls, people, guards, anything. I didn't see Tor's community yet. I still had hope, so I pushed my painful steps onward.

"That's her!" a gruff voice yelled from my right, making me stumble against a raised root. Two Dramens from the group that had surrounded Tor and me appeared. How did they find me? They rode on large horses, one black and white, the other a reddish-brown color, both galloping this way.

No, no, no.

I sprinted, running for safety. Of course, the clouds opened their water wrath upon the land. It's not like I could simply run from feral men and their beasts without the added crappy weather dooming me to struggle further. The rain made it harder to move quickly, but it also slowed down the horses barreling after me.

Red leaves formed in the peripheral vision to my right. The red tree.

The community was real.

If the tree existed, then everything else was real, too. I was so close. My boots dug into the wet earth harder as I pushed off, landing on the balls of my feet with renewed strength to run faster than I had before. This was it!

"Someone! Help!" I screamed for anyone at the gigantic tree to see me, anyone to help me from the two Dramens who were gaining on me quickly. The slopping sounds of hooves were getting closer.

"Help! Someone! Please!" I could see a double door in an intricately carved archway of the tree. It looked like the decoration of an old cathedral.

No one came forward, and I saw no walls around the large tree. My body slammed into the hard, wooden doors; they didn't budge. I tried to open them but they refused to move. My wet fingers gripped the handles and pulled hard before I saw the Dramens get off their horses to grab me.

"Come on. Please!" I screamed, violently trying to go past the magical doors to freedom.

Rough hands gripped me around the waist. I slipped out from them, the rain making me harder to hold onto.

"Let's go, girl. You've got no one else to save you." One of the Dramens smirked, his lips pierced, and his brown dreads made him look menacing. Even his partner, while staying silent, promised awful things with the way his stare lingered on the soaked, see-through clothes clinging to my body.

"Never." I gripped my sword, the only weapon I could carry. Everything else I'd ditched to run farther and faster. Any unnecessary weight was now scattered across the land I'd crossed.

If no one was coming for me, then I'd just have to fight until I died. At least this tree looked like a beautiful place to share a last breath. Maybe that was the safe haven all along. Not a community full of people, but a place for a peaceful death.

I raised my sword, ready to strike, showing these two creatures I was not simply a survivor waiting to be plucked up for their liking. I'd killed two of their kind and sliced another. I was a warrior.

Just as I started to swing toward the two men, a bright light glared from behind me, like I was the angel of death coming for the Dramens. Arrows slammed into their chests, and they fell to the ground with wide eyes on their dead faces.

My body shifted toward the light . . . to once-closed doors that were now open.

Chapter Eight

I wasn't expecting an outrageous warm welcome with banners and rose petals being thrown before my feet after having traveled so far. I definitely didn't think I would have been bound, hands behind my back, some cloth thrown over my head, and then carried on someone's shoulder to the unknown.

It wasn't a Dramen haven. They would have been rougher with me and pushed me in the elegant tree door instead of trying to pull me away from it. I fought as best as I could, kicking and writhing to free my hands from the rope behind my back, except it was useless. Whoever these people were, they didn't care that I kept trying to tell them that I was a survivor and that I wouldn't hurt them.

At first, one of the people who bound me huffed and sounded like an annoyed male. He murmured something about me walking too slow and then a shoulder dug in my gut before I was thrown over a large muscular body.

My body crashed hard on a solid surface as the man dumped me on the ground without easing the fall. So much for relaxing and soothing my muscles once I found the community. Instead, I was thinking how the hell I could get out of here.

The bag was suddenly pulled off my head. The growl that I'd planned on releasing unto these assholes stuck in my throat. I lost the ability to speak.

The room was large and natural, as if they'd built this magnificent place with nature, not on top of it. There were dimmed lights from the torches strewn along white columns in a pattern leading up to a magnificent wood-carved throne. Stunned from the beauty, I didn't even try to rise from the solid ground.

A large tree bloomed behind the dais, glowing from an opened ceiling giving way for the moonlight to create prisms in what looked like crystal leaves. Rainbows danced across the room, like they did from a disco ball. It was like a dream.

I searched for something familiar, but there was nothing besides the ground beneath me. These were not Dramens, nor were they like any survivors I'd ever met. The people were dressed in an assortment of colors and not in clothes I'd seen anywhere other than fairy tale books back at Mariam's house—long flowing gowns of cotton and silk, exposing shoulders, torsos, and long lean legs. Everyone looked gorgeous, youthful, and unmarred by the harsh times of the world.

"Rise before Queen Olyndria, human." A short man approached me from the throne.

No, he was not a man. My limbs found their strength and my voice returned at the sight of the . . . the . . . I don't even know what he was, if it was even a "he."

I screamed and pushed my way backward on the floor, trying to flee from the creature before me. He was green and frumpy, with tusks growing from his large fish lips. His eyes were beady and brown. His hands grasped a short staff with a rounded river stone on the top, wrapped in the bark. He dressed himself in pants, a simple white shirt that did nothing to hide his round belly, and a leather brown vest. If I had to guess, I would think he was a mixture between a warthog and a frog. His feet looked like they may be webbed, but I wasn't sure.

Was I dead? Oh God, what if the Dramens had killed me and Tor.

Tor was with them. I'd failed him. The little green creature huffed in frustration and took a step forward.

"The Queen awaits you. Hush your screams, child. Let's get this over with."

I stopped freaking out to look around for help, my sight going back and forth from the warthog-frogman to the crowd who watched me with curiosity. It hit me like a bucket of ice-cold water on a hot day. My panic ceased, and I stared at the thing speaking before me.

"Did you just say Queen Olyndria?"

Tor's stories were about a Fae queen named Olyndria. I couldn't accept what my ears had heard. It couldn't be, could it? My hands shook as the thoughts of the impossible raced across the realm of my imagination into possibility.

"Yes. Now, please stand." His eyes rolled, and despite his frustration, he obviously had to be polite to me. His thumping foot and grim mouth spoke more than his words about his feelings.

I couldn't find the queen on the gloriously carved throne. Where was she? I scrambled to my feet, needing to know, needing to see the queen for myself.

The creature nodded, content with my rising to stand. He gestured with his staff to follow him. There were two men, dressed as guards with armor, behind me. With every step I took, they followed, ready to confine me or slice my head off with their shiny swords at their tapered waists.

A few feet next to the throne, among a small gathering of people, was the queen, a breathtakingly beautiful woman. She hadn't noticed me yet, as she murmured with an equally gorgeous man with black hair and three savage pink scars down the right side of his face that skipped over his eye like someone had burned those lines. It looked brutal yet didn't take away from his beauty.

The queen captivated me. I was enamored by her presence. Her pale skin shimmered like she'd brushed herself with diamond dust, her long, wavy, brown hair glistened softly underneath a crown of six-inch-long crystals. I guessed they were diamonds around her head. Her golden dress caressed the tops of her toes and appeared modest, unlike some of the other clothes worn around this place.

"My Queen, we had a human at tree door," Frog-pigman announced to the queen. Gasps were heard around the room, and the scarred man turned to me. Only indifference and maybe a smudge of disgust crossed his features as he sneered.

The queen's attention shifted to where I stood. She was so beautiful, so elegant, and so Fae. I couldn't deny the reality in front of me, especially with the pointed ears. Tor hadn't just been telling me stories . . . he had told me history.

Fae were real, and I landed right in the middle of a magical world.

Chapter Nine

Tor told me that Queen Olyndria was mad, driven crazy after using her power to keep her daughter safe in a tomb of onyx. This Fae woman did not look mad at all. She faced me; her features softened. Her smile did not reveal teeth, but at least it wasn't like the sneer of the dark-haired man she stood beside who would not stop glaring in my direction.

Her mouth parted, and my whole body hummed. I wanted to hear her speak; I needed to hear her speak with every beat of my human heart.

"Cats and owls, tweedles and tulips. Tick, tock, tick, tock. Moon is here."

That was . . . well . . . not what I was expecting to come from a queen of the Fae. Maybe she was mad, speaking like a crazy person. A petite figure whose face was half-covered by a hood and who was dressed in an elegant blue-and-white robe nodded, as if he knew what the queen had said.

"Take her to Celestine, Turgen." A female voice spoke beneath the hood to the green creature before me.

Turgen nudged me with his staff to walk toward the two guards behind us. A silver shimmer coated the queen's eyes, and tears formed against her brown lashes and porcelain skin.

My chest ached, seeing her emotion. I didn't know if they were good or bad tears that rolled down the queen's cheek. The scarred man beside her growled when he noticed the queen crying, then sneered at me again.

I began to speak, remembering why I had arrived here, and what I needed to do. Turgen shushed me and pushed my body toward a grand door.

"You do not speak, vermin, until we say so." Quietly, the guards walked me away. As we traveled, an onslaught of emotions hit me. My mind was a jumble of mixed thoughts, with so many questions as to what was happening.

We exited the palace, which was made of large, exquisitely carved wood woven together like in a cathedral. Stained glass, artwork, and nature breathed into every facet of the architecture.

"Enough gawking, you worm." He nudged me so hard with his stick that my right knee buckled and I fell into a thick bush. Embarrassment and anger heated my face. I was going to knock that little green shit into the past.

Thrashing and flailing to get out of the bushes, I saw the world around me. The sky was dark, with the light from the crescent moon shining brightly, illuminating every blade of grass. Stars decorated the darkness above, as if the whole galaxy could be seen in just this small view between the giant trees. Jagged mountains peaked with white caps of snow appeared in the distance. A small river coursed through the large city. Fae and creature alike were going about their business, although not as many as I would have expected. Since it was also only night, most were probably asleep.

Shops and huts were made out of various materials of nature—stone, wood, or the trunks of trees. Torches and little orbs of bluish light scattered across the cobblestone roads. This was a safe haven, away from the Dramens, a place to simply be and hopefully do as I wished.

It seemed humans weren't particularly liked here so for now, I'd play along, see what they wanted, and get a good scope of my surroundings. Once we talked to this Celestine, I would figure out my course of action. Though tired, I followed the guards and my dearest green escort past the brighter lights of the city, off the main roads, and down to what looked like a cave.

Tor never mentioned anything about cave trolls in his stories, so I crossed my fingers behind my back, hoping I was not being thrown to some creature to become its dinner.

"I'm very malnourished. Whatever monster you are taking me to won't want me. They might even turn on you. You're plump. Obviously the better choice." I tried to walk with confidence instead of letting the fear take over all of me like it had in my belly.

The creature snarled as we trudged into the cave. Flickers of light danced on the stone ceiling without torches. *Was it an illusion?*

"You go alone," he growled and smacked my leg with his staff. The pain radiated up my thigh and threatened to drop me on the cave floor.

"Hit me again with that stick, and I'm going to kick your little green butt across the mountains." I reached for Turgen, ready to grip him by the shirt but he was already walking back toward the entrance and most likely, only exit.

A breeze of lavender-scented wind came from the inner parts of the cave, sweeping past me and soothing my mind despite the terror in my mind.

"Sapphira." The wind beckoned me. Toward Celestine. I knew if I tried to run out of the cave, they'd only toss me back in. I had no choice but to venture farther into the unknown.

I took a deep breath and followed the calming scent around a few stone corners, observing the carvings in the rock. I saw gems, people with pointed ears, a tree with crystals like the one in the throne room, two wolves, one much larger than the other, and a hand inside fire. There were others as I passed through an archway and into a room with a fire. Owls sat on tree branches, the open woods behind them. It was not a cave I had ventured through but maybe a tunnel.

"I almost thought you'd never take those final steps inside, Sapphira. Of course, I knew you would, though. Stubborn, stubborn." A woman's voice came from where the owls sat, their tails wagging.

I stopped moving. Owls didn't have tails to wag, and there was a large form sitting on the branch with the owls that I didn't notice before. Both the fire and moonlight weren't enough to see what the large shadow appeared to be.

"Who are you?" I demanded. My hands clenched, in case I needed to fight.

The shadow dropped to the ground and a woman with dark-as-night hair popped up. It was almost hard to distinguish where the ebony sky ended and her straight short hair began. Her skin was pale as the moonlight, and her body was not thin like the rest of the Fae I had seen in the city.

"Who are you?" I asked again. This time the woman smiled, her teeth flashing and her eyes wide like an owl. It was unnerving the way she shifted and looked around, then back at me. I wanted to recoil and cover myself with my arms to keep her from seeing into my soul.

"I'm Celestine. Seer of the Fae. Keeper of destinies."

Chapter Ten

Celestine was not going to eat me.

Instead, she made me tea and gave me a delicious meal of what I hoped was chicken, cooked carrots, and bread. My belly ached from eating so much but I couldn't stop myself from devouring everything, even if I ended up being sick.

Celestine patiently waited while I gobbled every crumb of food and drank her tea, as the owls with ears and tails like cats perched near her and walked against her legs.

This was her home, I think. The wooden stool she sat on in front of me was old and worn from use, and pots were scattered around the old tree to my right. I had no idea where the rest of her belongings were, and I was slightly nervous to look or ask.

Once I finished, I settled against the grass and sipped the rest of the tea, gathering the strength to talk to her and answer whatever questions she had for me. I had been pushed into here for a reason, and I suspected that whatever I was going to learn here would change me forever.

"Wonderful. I see a little color returning to your cheeks already, my dear." She placed her tea down on the ground and continued to look me over with those strangely wide owl eyes.

"Thank you. It's been a while since I ate so much food," I admitted and my full stomach agreed with me.

"The tea will help with the cramping you might have gotten from the fullness." As if her words were magic, my body relaxed, easing into a comfortable state without any aches. Even my legs appeared to have discharged the soreness that had begun to lock up my limbs.

"I know you have some questions. Out with them, so that you may get some rest before dawn." I nodded toward her. I had so many questions, so many thoughts.

"Do you really know everything? Like the future?" Maybe it was lame to ask this first, but I wanted to know what being a seer meant.

She nodded and the owl at her foot hooted. It also sounded like a meow. There were so many mixtures of animals in this place.

"I do not see anymore. Not for some time now. I had seen them before, when magic was as real as the blood beating in your heart." Her pale hand reached up to touch her chest, as if she could feel the magic inside there, like a phantom pulse beneath her skin.

"So, it's true then. The stories Tor told me. The Fae have no magic anymore. King Verin, Olyndria, the princess. All of it is true?" I wanted to believe before. I'd been in Tor's arms and dreamed of this world. Even here . . . now where I could smell and taste it . . . doubt lingered.

"Yes, and you play a very important part in this story. Tor was sent to find you and bring you here for a reason, my dear."

"Tor was sent to find me? He knew this was real?" I was on my feet instantly, pacing back and forth on the grass.

"This may hurt, child. I see that. But yes. I sent Tor to find you and bring you here. Despite what you think of yourself, you will play a part in the breaking of the onyx and releasing the savior into this world." Celestine didn't sugarcoat things, and while I appreciated it, I still couldn't believe it. Tor kept this from me. He made me believe these were just fantasy stories of the Fae. Not history.

The shaking of my head in disbelief turned to laughter.

"I am no one in this story, let alone some hero who will help save the world." I was human, and I was lacking in the skills some mighty superhero would have. There was no way I could take on an army and I definitely had no power to break a tomb of onyx. Hell, if these Fae and creatures hadn't been able to do it, then I didn't stand a chance.

"You are everything," she insisted, and I scoffed. I was not everything, I was only me.

"You will stay here in Crysia. And you will train. You will learn everything you can, and then you will rescue Prince Tor from those evil heathens in one month's time." She stood and her stare held no room for argument. I was being told what I would do, and that was that.

"Prince Tor?" My thoughts swirled fast in my head.

"Tor is also known as Prince Torin, heir to the throne across the sea, and betrothed to the princess. He is half-Fae and human, the bridge between our worlds, and was the only one who could find you and bring you here without anyone knowing our realm exists. I am sorry, dear. I know what he means to you. You must not give up, and in one month you will go get him back. He sacrificed himself for you. You will not let that sacrifice go in vain. He believed in you, as do I."

"These people are not just going to let me stay here. They look at me as if I am a bug on their boots."

Celestine smiled, knowing for now I accepted what she said as truth. It was the part about Tor's sacrifice that got me the most. He did that for me, a half-Fae prince. I owed him everything. He had saved me many times before and made sure I was going somewhere safe. Despite the unknown settings around me, I began to feel at ease.

"A bargain will be struck; you will stay in the palace as a servant in exchange for your training. If you had reached a normal human community instead of Crysia, you would have done the same thing. Bartered shelter in exchange for work. This is no different. You will be given clothes, shelter, and food. The people of the courts won't bother you because most of them wouldn't look down to a servant unless something was needed." She made me another cup of tea and handed it over gently.

I was not a drinker of spirits and alcohol like some were back where I used to live, but after the day I'd had, I wished I could drink something a little stronger than tea.

"I still don't think I can do this, but I will do what I can to save Tor," I vowed, even if he was to marry another woman if I somehow succeeded in breaking that onyx tomb holding the princess inside.

I laughed to myself. Memories started to make sense. He was promised to another. No wonder he never wanted to take our relationship further than kissing.

Except . . . where did this leave our love? Would I be able to save him, then watch him be with someone else?

"Drink the tea dear, and when you wake, it will be a new day with the world at your feet."

I'd already started drinking, so by the time her words registered in my head, I was already falling asleep. My eyelids lost their battle to stay open, and the cup clattered to the ground as I slept.

Chapter Eleven

I slept long and deep. My muscles were tight, as I sat up in the unfamiliar room. The soreness I'd expected from the journey was gone, and for once, I felt rested.

What the hell was in the tea?

I looked at my surroundings. I'd been moved from beside Celestine's fire and had no idea who did it or what happened. I scanned my body and clothes for any signs of hostility but was met with the same dirty set of cotton and skin I had before. I sighed in relief.

One month.

Celestine said I had one month to gather my strength, train, and then I was to rescue Tor, which meant he was alive. Not wanting to waste any more time, I hopped off the bed, stronger and ready to do what I had to do. My stomach rumbled, and I realized I needed food and had to clean up before I left this barren room.

It was small. There was enough space for a single sleeper bed, a table next to it with a cup of what looked to be water. Then across the stone floor was a fireplace with dancing flames giving off heat and a stone-carved circle that appeared to be a tub and toilet next to it. This was better than the ground and leaves I'd been dealing with for weeks to relieve myself. There were buckets of water near the fire, so hopefully I had hot water, though I didn't let myself become too attached to the idea of a hot bath.

I rushed to the tub, hoping I would have enough time to clean myself thoroughly, since it had been a while since I'd washed myself in anything other than a river.

The water was lukewarm but better than nothing. Wasting no time, I undressed, got into the tub and threw the smaller buckets of water on my head. Raised flesh from the change in temperature made me shiver for only a moment before I grabbed a rag and what I hoped was soap from the side of the tub. With every scrub of the rag on my skin, I cleaned off every touch of the Dramens and the dry air from the desert. Regretfully, I also cleaned off Tor's touch.

A bang on the solid door made me jump and clear my thoughts away from Tor.

"Be out this door in five minutes." A man's bellow echoed inside the room.

I finished scrubbing my face and rinsed my hair before climbing out of the tub to dry myself. There was a three-foot-wide, six-foot-tall wardrobe that I hoped held my salvation. My fingers gripped the wood. It wasn't carved or held any extra embellishments like I'd seen everywhere else. The inside did have a towel sitting on a little shelf and four unusual outfits.

There was another bang on the door, signaling the man's impatience. Whoever he was, he could wait a few more seconds for me to get dressed. I dried off as quickly as I could and grabbed the first thing I saw on a hanger. The new clothes were simple and soft. A long-sleeved green dress slit at the hips became one piece of material in the front and back. I grabbed some pants, since my thighs would be exposed in the dress. They were snug against my legs like leggings but did not have as much stretch to them. I tugged on the black slippers from the bottom of the wardrobe. I wrapped a scarf-like belt around my waist to keep everything together instead of looking like I had a blanket simply thrown over me. There was no mirror to check how I looked, so I hoped my attire was presentable. My skin was clean and my hair would air-dry as the day went on.

I pulled the door open and hurried out, only to collide with a hard, muscular chest covered in a black shirt. My feet stumbled back slightly as my gaze lifted from the muscular torso, up a tanned corded neck, then up past a sharp clean-shaven jaw, and finally landing on scars. It was the Fae who had sneered at me while standing next to Queen Olyndria yesterday.

"Took you long enough," he barked. His icy-blue eyes narrowed before he turned and walked down the hall. I closed my door and hustled the few feet after him.

"I hate to sound cliché here, but who are you and where are we going?" I chased after him, my tired legs having trouble keeping up with his long, confident stride.

He huffed without a backward glance or actual words.

"I assume Celestine told someone what's going on before she drugged me to sleep?" The halls we walked through were quiet. I tried to take in as much as I could while making sure I didn't get lost. However, the Fae male was on a mission to get me somewhere and he wasn't dallying.

There was no huff this time or any sound from his large body.

Sparing the man a second glance, I decided he had to be some sort of warrior or fighter. His body was all muscle beneath his simple clothes, with a sword attached to his hip. His black hair was cut short but not too short. There was something about him. He was stoic, and his sneer was the only part of his face I would consider ugly.

We walked through the empty throne room. Our footsteps echoed around the white columns. The crystal tree blew in some unknown wind I couldn't feel. The rainbows once again danced across the ground and walls from the sunlight reflected through the facets.

There were two heavily armored guards standing by a solid, arched wooden door with no carvings on it. They nodded as soon as they saw the man leading me in their direction and stepped aside, opening the door as they did.

The man walked into the room and abruptly turned on his heel to face me, his face menacing and angry. He radiated hatred, which I hadn't earned. Moments ago, I had thought he was the most beautiful man I'd ever seen, even with the three scars running down his face, marring his skin. But this attitude made him ugly.

"I'm gonna tell you this now, and then there will be no more need for talking beyond you doing as I say, when I say it. My name is Rune, and I'm going to be training you. I don't give two damns about you, where you come from, or what great love you have for my brother. Celestine is a hag who likes to meddle. The only reason I am doing this is for her." His long, callused finger pointed toward an onyx tomb.

The onyx tomb. The real-life scene from Tor's stories. I remembered all those nights that I dreamt of a princess asleep in the dark crystal, waiting to be released.

"Celestine says that you are the one to free her. Make no mistake. We will not be friends. You will hate me as time goes on, but you will become stronger and you will save her."

Princess Nyx lay lovingly in jagged onyx, sharp points sparkling from the skylight above her, shining down, just like Tor had described. The onyx was massive, probably as big as one of the larger SUVs I'd seen decaying on the roads. Both the onyx and the purple-haired goddess were beautiful.

I looked at the man who had brought me, his eyes staring at the princess. I understood his gaze on her, his longing. I knew the emotion deep in my chest . . . the ache to touch someone you loved but couldn't.

Tor was promised to marry Princess Nyx, and Rune, his apparent brother loved her, while I loved Tor.

Fuck.

Chapter Twelve

My first day in Crysia, the Fae realm of the West, was exhausting.

Rune quickly moved us from where his sleeping princess lay to the kitchen where he tossed me a few pieces of jerky, then we walked to a field by the base of a waterfall just outside the palace. There were no shops or homes, just an open space where the sounds of my panting and screams couldn't be heard over the water falling off the edge and colliding with the river below.

I showed Rune what I knew, things Tor had taught me. He rolled his eyes more than a few times. I tried to hit Rune, I really did. Every punch I threw, he dodged quickly. Every kick or tackle I tried to make he took a step to the side, knowing where I was going to attack. With every miss, his aggravation grew. It was like every chance I failed was a step farther away from being reunited with the woman he loved.

I grumbled once that I hoped she truly was the savior of this world and that this was worth it.

I should have known better than to have spoken my thoughts aloud. Rune punished me for the action by giving me an impossible task. I had to climb the stone wall beside the waterfall. Slick rocks and moss were not the only obstacle in my way. I had no strength in my upper body to do that, let alone the fear that coated my insides at the thought of falling.

"Do it!" he barked, his body posture rigid, and his big arms crossed over his chest expectantly.

I tried. I only made it about five feet off the ground before he yelled, his voice as powerful as the falls itself.

"Do it again!"

And again. And again. Every time I fell, I got back up and tried over and over. We paused for a moment to eat, then I was back to trying to hit him. My body stung like it was going to splinter apart at the seams. I needed more rest; I needed more food. I lacked muscle and nutrients. My body needed the time to adjust from one survival mode to another.

After Rune finished trying to kill me with training, I was sentenced to cleaning the palace as needed to earn my keep. The other servants were quiet as Rune passed his babysitting duties onto them before he stormed off to probably make some other person's day miserable. Shortly after the awkward introductions, I was put on floor duty.

None of the other servants talked to me much beyond showing me where I was to work, what tools I'd use, and where to put everything once I was done. The Fae who passed me ignored me, as their steps brought more dirt onto my freshly cleaned floors.

Thankfully, Celestine kept her promise of not telling many people the purpose of my presence. However, the pressure of my task built inside me like a stone in a river weighing me down more with every step.

At least the people in my community where I'd grown up were kind. Tor was kind, and the fact that he was half-Fae and part of this realm spoke much more for the Fae than they realized. If he was so good, then there were more just like him. I was sure of it.

Servants were supposed to be quiet. They received a small salary to do their jobs and go home. Since I was living here, my salary was my rent. It would have been nice to earn a wage, but I had a safe place to live. Hopefully one day I'd get to explore Crysia further and see the shops and land I'd glanced at through my window.

When the day was done, I'd settled in my new room with a plate of roast beef and potatoes. "Tomorrow is a new day, Sapphira," I muttered to myself, exhausted, missing the companionship of Tor in the quiet moments. I anticipated another day of aching muscles, pain, and most likely a grumpy Rune. I'd seen him a few times after our training had ended, but he ignored me, like I wasn't even there.

As I ate, I thought of Tor and his brother. There was so many things I didn't know. What was their relationship like? Was Rune the older brother? Where did he get his scars from? Why didn't Tor mention his brother in the stories?

Both were tall and had blue eyes but the similarities ended there. Tor was kind, and he made me laugh. His smile brightened my day and oozed warmth.

He was comfortable and safe. I never tired of his voice and had loved those moments when he told me stories to help me sleep. His blue gaze surrounded me like a blanket warmed by the sun. Rune's glacial look was like having a bucket of arctic water thrown on your head. Rune had been forged as a warrior. One brother was born and bred for war. The other maybe a diplomat? Tor would marry the princess as a way to grow the two kingdoms together harmoniously. Tor would be king, loved by everyone who had the pleasure of being in his presence. Tor was likeable, unlike Rune.

I set my empty plate on the small table next to the little bed and sighed. Celestine said I would be learning their history as well as physical training. That was something I was elated to do. There was so much to see and experience here.

But I knew my purpose. I couldn't laze around. I had a job to do: learn the skills necessary to save Tor and free Princess Nyx while taking care of the palace I was housed in.

I prayed I had the strength to do it.

I'd save Tor, and I'd try to save the princess. If I failed, Rune might lock me in the onyx room until I found a way or died trying.

Chapter Thirteen

The next few days passed in the same manner as my first day did. I dressed in clothes, much like the ones I had before, then made a mental note to talk to someone about where I would clean the ones I'd gotten dirty. I trained with a cranky Rune. Muscles I didn't even know I had hurt from having not being used before, like the area beneath the back of my arms and my ribs. The pain jolted me every time I mopped and moved a rag.

The lead servant of the palace pitied me and moved me to kitchen duty. There I helped peel at least a hundred potatoes and carrots and shucked corn. There always seemed to be a gathering in the throne room at night. The Fae loved to entertain one another and talk about the local gossip of Crysia.

I was getting changed for bed in a simple tunic when someone banged on my door, loudly enough to make me jump off the bed in fright.

No guesses as to who it was. I already knew it was Rune.

"What?" I opened the door, grouchy and tired.

He wore his cream-colored tunic and black pants with a leather belt he had worn earlier today. No weapons could be seen, though I'd found out in our session Rune didn't need them. He was faster than anyone, and he was strong.

I wasn't on his time right now. I could act as I pleased. We both knew I wasn't going anywhere. Even if I tried, he would drag me back in hopes I would rescue his love.

"Tomorrow you're going to be in the library," he said.

"Great. A nice break from my excellent trainer will do me some good," I retorted, ready to shut the door in his face.

He walked away. Stupid jerk. Stupid stonehearted, icy-eyes jerk. I let out an exasperated groan and closed the door. At least tomorrow would be a change from what I'd experienced so far. Since my new meeting place was in the library, I assumed I would be learning about the Fae's history.

Quickly, I sat on my bed and blew out the candle on the nightstand. The fire in the fireplace would give me a little light and keep the room from the cool breeze outside. There was a small window by my bed, and I liked to look out to the city and the woods behind it. Even with the darkness, the moonlight was bright enough that I saw the leaves rustling in the wind.

A large black shadow sailed in the sky. As quickly as it came, it was gone.

There were so many mysteries to solve. However, before I solved anything, I needed rest. I needed to heal from today, hoping tomorrow I wouldn't be doing anything physical beyond picking up a book.

**

I didn't sleep very long, and I was oddly grateful for the early rise. I'd put the buckets of water closer to the fire last night, hoping they would warm up nicely so I could soak in the tub before starting my day. I was adjusting to this life, both mentally and physically.

There were moments I wanted to bolt and run as fast as my tired feet could carry me, but then I remembered I was not some weakling. I would not give up. I didn't die in the apocalypse, and I wouldn't die now.

The bath was every bit as wondrous as I'd been dreaming of during my travels to arrive here. My aches calmed, as well as the stress in my head. Everything melted away.

Then the banging began.

I cursed loudly enough for him to hear me. It was like he knew I was trying to relax, to let my frustration toward him flow out of me into the swirling water going down the drain when I pulled the plug.

With a growl, I grabbed my drying sheet to wrap around my dripping body and opened the door.

"What is your deal?" I leveled Rune with a fiery stare, attempting to incinerate him where he stood for ruining the moment I'd been dreaming of for weeks. Months!

The smirk on his face promised he would attempt to rattle me or piss me off, as I stood with water falling to the ground in little splashes from my body. Pink blush coated my cheeks as I thought about how inappropriate this was, but I wasn't backing down now. He would only use this as fuel for later if I showed any signs of vulnerability.

"The queen wanted to see you after the library for tea." His nostrils flared, and his face hardened as he turned to leave, his sharp jaw twitching with anger.

Poor Princess Nyx, the prime focus of his love. I bet he wouldn't even know what to do with someone he cared about. Grunt and yell at them? No thanks.

Despite thinking him a jerk, I watched as he stomped down the hall. What happened to him that made him so . . . prickly. However, I'd probably be punished if I asked about his personal life so I stepped back into my room to shut the door, leaving those thoughts on the other side.

It wasn't worth jumping back in the bath anymore. My mind was awake and reeling. I dried myself, careful not to slip on the wet spots I'd created earlier. Hopefully I wouldn't be doing anything physical today to mess up my appearance so I could look at least halfway decent when having tea with the queen.

The only outfit I had left was an off-the-shoulder, long-sleeved purple tunic held up by a brown vest tied in the front, which showed off the little bit of womanly curve I did have, and some of the softest brown leggings I'd ever worn.

Eagerly wanting to feel the material against my newly cleansed skin, I hurried into the clothes and threw on the slippers I was given. A few random strings sat in my wardrobe that I had no idea what they were for, so I grabbed one and used it to tie my messy curls in a bun on top of my head.

"It's a new day. Gonna be a great one," I whispered to myself, the walls, and whatever creatures within hearing range.

I'd dusted near the library for an hour yesterday, so as soon as I shut the door to my room, I headed to it with ease and no escort.

Freedom at last.

Chapter Fourteen

As I meandered the stone passages, the halls bustled with excitement about a ball tonight.

I wondered if it was the same type of ball I'd read about in fairy tale books as a child with fancy dresses, dancing, music, and a glorious feast. I knew I would not be invited, though it would have been nice to see. We had some dancing nights at the community in the past. I'd dance to the strumming of a guitar or a harmonica that Mark, one of the men, used to play. We never played anything too loud so we wouldn't attract the Dramens' attention. I'd get dolled up in one of the only dresses I'd owned, a pretty blue sundress that reached my knees. We'd eat food and celebrate being alive in the warmer season after having survived the cold months.

Maybe I'd sneak down to the ball and take a look or offer myself as the help to clean tables and hold trays of food. Anything to see what happened at a Fae gathering. I bet their outfits would be breathtaking, with beautiful colors swirling around the rainbow-hued throne room or out in the garden, where there was a stream and flowers.

I'd been daydreaming so thoroughly, I didn't pay attention to where I walked and ran into someone. At first, I thought it was Rune. It would be just my luck he would catch me daydreaming. It wasn't him.

It was a pale-white, almost-gray Fae with big blue eyes like Celestine's . . . owlish. Her hair was pale and seemed to float in the air like the smoke of a snuffed-out candle. Her fingers were long with pointed claws at the end of the tips. Shimmers of what looked like feathers in her skin mesmerized me.

"I'm so sorry." I bent down to help pick up the books she'd been holding, now strewn about on the floor. Her head tilted to the side, like she was trying to understand me.

Her petite body and pointy facial features also reminded me of Celestine.

"I'm Celestine's niece, Myandris. But you can call me Dris." Her voice was soft, like she didn't want the louder vibrations of her sound to disturb the books around us. Everything about her said soft and reserved despite the wild, wavy, fluffed-out hair. Her long dress had been dyed light blue, and it stopped just under her knees. She wasn't wearing any shoes. Her toes looked like her fingers, shimmering, with pointed claws.

"I'm—" I tried to say my name while handing her the three books.

"You're Sapphira. Human who is going to free us. I've been excited to meet you. Celestine spoke highly of you. That's why I'm going to try to teach you everything I can. Oh, this is so exciting, being a part of something bigger than yourself, you know. Well . . ." She blushed. "I know you know. You're like a hero. A human doing all this for us and your world."

I was taken aback by the compliment and her excitement. "Thanks. Do you see things, too?" I was curious if her aunt was the only one who had the gift.

She shook her head quickly. "No, that's all her. She's the only one who can. But I do know a lot of things. I am the librarian here. Please, come follow me. I've set out a bunch of books for us at a table. I can't wait to get started." If her feet weren't clearly on the floor, I would have thought she floated into the library.

I'd seen the library in passing yesterday, and while it wasn't a grand room like the ballroom, it was still beautiful. There were six tables in the middle of the tiled floors, one stacked with books. Two stories were covered in floor-to-ceiling books. The stairs and railings were carved wood, thick and sturdy. The breathtaking ceiling had magnificent paintings of magic, the queen, Fae in battle, and Fae embraced in lovers' arms. A dragon and a firebird flew across the library as if traveling from one book to another. The arched windows let in the natural sunlight. I didn't want to look away.

"There's lots of history up there. Every piece of art carries a tale to be told around here," Dris said.

"It's very beautiful here. Where I come from, there isn't much like this anymore. The Dramens don't care about beauty unless it breeds or makes them coins." I hated saying their name in this place, like it would seep from of my lips and stain the elegance.

"I've heard about them but never ran into one. Only a certain few have." She organized the books to her liking as I grabbed the wooden chair to sit.

"How is it this place exists and hasn't been tainted by them?" I had thought that question over and over. I saw no walls or anything that would keep them out by the door in the red tree. The Dramens had to have walked all over those woods looking for food or people. I couldn't figure it out.

"We are in a different realm than them, and the only portals are ones we guard heavily. They don't know about it. I think this is a great place to start your lessons about how we and the humans coexisted."

I settled into my seat, tense but eagerly waiting for Dris to tell me everything. "Great! I feel so lost and don't know anything."

She smiled happily. "The Fae have been around for many millennia. The exact details of our history like where we came from have been lost to our historians for a very long time, but there are some that say we came from a tree. When its seeds fell into the Earth, it created life. Some of us were granted the gift of nature from our mother tree. However, no tree has been found in our realm, so I wouldn't put much thought into that theory. We do have nature cores, though."

Tor had said every Fae had a core or soul of nature. "The gems are royalty, right?" I asked, hoping to show her I wasn't completely clueless. She nodded, holding no judgment for my knowledge.

"Yes. Gems are royal. Our queen has a core of a diamond. She was the most powerful being in our realm. The second is a rare core of a dragon."

A dragon. My mouth must have dropped because Dris giggled and continued on.

"There are many magical creatures in the realm. Dragons used to be one of them, although everyone believes them to be extinct. Unicorns, firebirds, werewolves, and other incredible creatures still lurk about in the woods. I've seen the unicorn herds a few times. They are a very skittish group and don't like to be looked at much. Can't say I blame them. Vanity isn't everything."

I hoped secretly I would get the chance to see one in my lifetime.

"Our job, as Fae, was to keep these creatures and other dangerous Fae from entering your world through our gates and wreaking havoc. Only a few chosen humans knew about what we did. That's why our gates are in the national parks, where no one can destroy them." She finished organizing and her pointed fingers ran over the map on the table gently.

"There are three portals to the human realm, each near a large city. Ours, which you found in Yosemite, is called Crysia. We are a people of leaders, protectors, and hope. We value nature, rhythm, and symbiosis—living together to make our world a better place for everyone, from the tiny little bunnies to the great queen. Everyone coexists and works together.

Across the land, you'll find many little villages. Everyone gets along fine for now and there are trade routes that keep industry moving. On the other side of the continent as you know it is a city of intelligence, truth, and the arts and sciences. Crystoria. They have the largest and most beautiful library." Dris's focus slipped as she dreamed of Crystoria.

During her fantasy moment, I wondered if I'd passed the portal to the city in my travels. Why did Tor bring me to this place, crossing over so much territory and peril with Dramens?

"Where is that one?" My curiosity held no use to me unless I voiced it.

"In the Great Smoky Mountains. You must see their architecture one day." I frowned. More questions . . . always more questions than answers. "You said there are three. Where is the other?"

Her lips scrunched together in distaste. "The badlands. That is where King Verin and his army remain, feasting on fear and chaos."

She shivered, bringing her hands up to rub her arms like she was fighting away a chill.

"Tor told me about him."

Her face went from downturned to elated in seconds. "Prince Tor. Oh, you knew him?" she cooed, as if in awe.

"Yeah, he's kind of my boyfriend."

Although, I wasn't sure if it was true anymore . . . a thought I tried not to obsess over.

"No way. He's so handsome. And smart. And did you know he once tamed a unicorn? Yes! It was a black stallion he named Mars," she gushed, her hands coming up to rest under her chin.

"I didn't know that. He is smart and handsome, though." My shoulders dropped forward, the desire to curl up from the feelings inside me taking over. How could love feel so close to betrayal right now?

"I'm sorry. I can see you care for him deeply. Let's get back to our history lesson before lunch. I know you have a date with the queen for tea. She has the loveliest tea set made out of diamonds."

Thoughts of Tor lingered, so I was happy for the distraction about Crysia, learning about the Fae realm, its inhabitants, and what happened to the magic that used to blossom in every nature core.

Chapter Fifteen

By lunchtime, my brain was tired from Dris's knowledge . . . maps of the area from the castle through the shop districts to where artisan trade happened, to the east where the Hallowstag Woods rested then ended with the mountains called the Crescent Sisters.

I was told all about the ways of the Fae nobles and Queen Olyndria.

No one called her the Mad Queen to her face, but whispers surrounded Her Majesty. She spoke in words only she and her most trusted advisor, Ryka, understood. She was still the queen by her diamond core and her marriage to King Lachan, and no one challenged her throne except Verin, who had disappeared during the apocalypse. His castle in the badlands bustled with chaos. Hordes of his army went on raids, much like the Dramens of my realm.

Rune was the half-brother to Prince Tor, and though he was considered a prince by blood, no one in his family except Tor claimed him. His title and birthright was stripped, so he left with Tor to come here. He was chosen by the queen to be the head of Crysia's army, and even I admitted he was a good fit. He was determined, focused, strong, and fast. I'd yet to land a blow on him in the few days I'd been here. Dris's information made me more curious about him. Why did his family disown him?

"I've heard that while he has a prickly personality, to those he values he is utterly devoted, loyal, and dare I say sweet?" She had leaned in to whisper the last part to me, which only made me giggle. Rune . . . nice? That really was something belonging in a fantasy world.

"Time to go." A gruff voice bounced off the tile floor, making my spine go rigid. Such perfect timing for him to show up when we were speaking about him.

"Hello, sweet Rune." I couldn't help poking him with my words and defiance. He made my life miserable, so I could do the same to him.

Twisting so I could get out of my chair, I looked him over with indifference and gestured for him to go so I could follow. His hand resting on the hilt of his sword gripped a little tighter. A small chuckle from behind me brought a smirk to my lips.

I thought I was on even ground with him at that moment, then of course I wasn't able to keep my metaphorical footing when those tightly pressed lips of his relaxed into a smirk of his own. *Shit.* I didn't know what kind of punishment I'd earned, but the look on his face said retribution was coming.

Without another word or glance at the Fae behind me, Rune walked out of the library.

"I'll see you in two days," I told Dris. I would come in for lessons every other day—one day training with the angry bear and then one day with her. The other hours of the day I'd spend earning my keep and savoring the sights of Crysia while I could.

Rune didn't speak as we turned corner after corner. I expected him to lead me toward the throne room. Instead he walked us out of the castle and to the waterfall where Rune loved to knock me on my ass. The queen sat on a large golden blanket with a variety of little sandwiches and fruits on crystal plates. The diamond tea kettle and cups shone in the sun's light, like a star beaming in the middle of the day.

"Majesty." He bowed at the waist to his queen. Her eyes crinkled with happiness, and her gentle smile indicated love. It was the type of greeting a family member would give. He spoke no more as he walked away.

Looking around to make sure this wasn't a trick, I noticed a sparkle by a tree in the distance of armor, and then another ten feet away from that one. Guards surrounded us just in case they thought I was a danger to her.

I wasn't. I only wanted to sit next to her and hear her voice, even if it was gibberish. Some inner part of me yearned for her approval. This was the queen of Tor's stories that I'd spent nights dreaming about. She'd fought in battles wearing golden armor with her brown hair braided back and a diamond crown on her head. She'd rallied her people together to constantly fight Verin, using her powers for good to save those beneath her. She was given great power and used it for her people. She went mad to give her daughter a fighting chance in the future.

Her brown eyes looked upon me and I grew heavy, like the weight of her world sat on my head. I could free her world from the onyx tomb, and this queen, whose loving smile made my world a little brighter, made me feel like I was the savior myself.

"Every fish has wings, and the trees do not lie. Fathers and water be here teatime." She hastily grabbed onto the handle of the kettle to pour the tea but it fumbled ungracefully and clattered against the teacups.

My hands scrambled over to pick up the kettle, grabbing one of the cloth napkins to blot out the spilled tea. The queen stared off into the waterfall, unfocused and unaware of what had happened. I did what I could to set everything back up as it was, and even took the liberty of pouring myself and her some tea.

"Thank you, your highness, for inviting me to tea. I've really wanted to meet you beyond those few moments when I first arrived. Crysia is beautiful." My words came out rushed as I then held my breath, hoping my words had reached her, wherever she'd gone in her mind.

It didn't work. She focused on the waterfall like she stared at the love of her life. Tears fell from her eyes, but there was no movement from her elegant form, no hitches in breath or redness of skin. It was like a statue of a fountain had sprung a leak. I didn't know what to say or do. I wanted to embrace the queen, except I didn't know if I'd get an arrow in my back if I tried.

"I never knew a place like this existed beyond the fairy tales I'd read as a child. It's wonderful what you've done here, and I can't wait to see more." The tea was warm as I took a sip and it tasted sweet, like it had drops of honey in it. I made myself a plate of the scrumptious sandwiches and one for her, as well.

She continued to stare at the waterfall and cry while I filled the void of sound on her part with my voice, telling her about myself and my life before I came here. I hoped she heard every word. Having a conversation was something I did when I was sad or stuck in my own head. It always made me feel better to listen to someone talk, even if they were simply reading a book. It usually brought me out my funk to think about something else. Maybe I could do that for her.

I ate, and she didn't touch her tea or food.

"Then we were attacked by Dramens. They were going to take me and most likely sell me but I got him with an axe that had been left in the old shed by the river." She moved and I squealed, my hand clenching my rapid-beating chest. She'd been still as stone for so many minutes that when she turned her head and began sipping her tea, I cursed. "Holy hell!" The cucumber sandwich in my hands dropped to the blanket.

The queen's gaze came up to meet mine, her body leaning closer, and her eyebrows drawn together. She looked at me as if danger was near, and she was ready to run or fight for me.

"So sorry. Everything is OK. I promise." I lifted my sandwich from the blanket and began eating it again. "See, nothing scary here. Everything is good." I smiled and tried to make everything appear like it was fine, but the little pinched line between her brows stayed until it was time for me to be escorted back.

Rune appeared, as if he'd been called by the wind to retrieve me. "The queen needs her rest. It's time to go." His voice was kinder with no bite in his words. His normally hardened jaw had softened. The queen glanced at him with a sweet smile, the type a mother would give her child.

My curiosity begged me to dig for information about their relationship. Did the queen know Rune was in love with her daughter? Was that the connection that had them acting like she was his family? So many thoughts swirled inside me as I stood to leave.

"Thank you for your time. I hope that we can do it again soon. I really enjoyed myself." I spoke the truth and did my best at a bow before strolling over to Rune. He watched me warily, probably wondering if I'd done something or pestered the queen.

The queen returned to staring into the cascading waterfall as if I was never there. Seeing her so broken, I wanted to cry. "Will she ever be OK?" I whispered to Rune once we were out of earshot, knowing that Fae hearing was better than humans.

"Some still have hope that when Nyx is released, it will reverse what has been done," he answered softly, without looking my way. I knew the hope in his words. He believed his love would be saved, and her mother would be fixed, too. He didn't need to say it; I could read between the lines.

"I'm sorry for your loss, Rune. The princess and the queen. I know you hate me for whatever reasons, but I really will try to save Tor and the princess."

I had extended an olive branch between us, but he didn't say anything as we headed to the kitchens for me to work until nightfall.

Chapter Sixteen

The ball was in full swing around midnight in the throne room. The rainbows reflecting from the swaying crystal tree painted the scene with magic, even though that element in this world was gone. I imagined what it was like before magic was lost: Fae using their gifts to their advantages to win friends or lovers or maybe to show their unique skills.

I was a wine girl for the night. Any Fae or creature who needed wine lifted a hand in the air and I'd rush over to pour some into a glass. As far as I could tell, Fae were like humans when it came to how they held their alcohol. Some could and some couldn't. Many slurred their words while others remained composed with a light pink flush coating their cheeks.

I learned a lot about the Fae through hands-on experience tonight. The Fae were a very sensual crowd, always touching each other, whether on the shoulder, the hand, or somewhere I'd rather pretend I didn't see. A few who didn't realize I wasn't Fae touched the tendrils of my messy curls that had popped out from the bun on my head or caressed my hand as I poured them a drink. Usually once they saw I didn't have pointed ears and slight canines in my mouth, they moved on. There were a few Fae who I could tell were troublemakers or pot stirrers as we liked to call them back home. I made sure to give them a wide berth in case they wanted to play a prank or cause harm in some way.

The queen was dressed in a glittering dark-blue ball gown. She looked like a gem herself, shining in the light, with her brown hair in waves to her lower back. She smiled and looked at people who talked to her sometimes. Everyone humored her, and it didn't sit well with me.

Rune was a no-show at the party, although I doubted he would enjoy something like this. A bubble of laughter escaped past my lips at the thought of grouchy Rune crowded by drunk females looking for attention or a dance with him. No doubt there would be blood.

Even with the unmentionables I'd seen at this ball, I still couldn't take my eyes away from everything. The music was entrancing, having never heard such instruments before. Men twirled women around, while the ladies smiled and moved like they'd been dancing together for centuries. The dresses were so many colors, and at a first glance looked like flowers floating over the floor, whirling in the wind. Some were scandalous, showing almost everything on both set of sexes. There were even couples off in the darker parts of the throne room making noises I'd rather not have heard, but no one seemed to care.

When Moriah, the head servant for the night, told me my services were done for the night, I almost told her I wanted to stay. However, I knew Rune would work me hard tomorrow. I needed to rest to have energy for training.

I walked down the halls, still hearing the echoes of the violin trailing after me. Looking to make sure no one watched, I swayed as I walked, moving my hands like I felt every note of the song against my fingers.

With my door in sight, I lifted my hands and twirled, pretending Tor led me. I bet he could dance like all the Fae at the ball with ease. He would know how to move, be cordial, and protect me from those who wanted to stir up trouble.

That was the Tor I knew, not the Prince Torin everyone else admired. As I reached my wooden door, I bowed, spun on one foot, and my servants' clothes spun with me. Once inside, I wiped myself down with a wet rag and soap and fell into bed with a smile on my face. Today had been a good day. Learning about the world I was now in helped me feel a little more secure in it, like this place wasn't going to pop like a bubble and I'd be lost. Doubts still lingered and thoughts wanted to barge into my happiness. For now, I pushed them back, and fell into the arms of sleep.

His face was damp, coated in dirt and days-old blood. They threw him inside an animal-skinned tent against the hard desert ground. He grunted and curled into a ball as the tall one kicked him in the gut with his hard-black boots.

"Don't hurt the man too much. He's got a pretty face. The queen might want him for herself." Another man with black paint and cruel eyes gazed upon the figure lying helplessly on the ground.

Tor.

He looked like he'd been dragged for miles, beaten, and starving.

"Oh, Tor," I called to him. I ran as fast as I could, then fell to my knees before him.

"I'm so sorry, Tor." Tears flowed down my cheeks as I reached out to push his brown hair back behind his ear, to see his face.

He groaned, his hands trying to get free from the confining rope. His eyes opened, and with barely any strength, he rose. He was trying to fight, even now when all seemed lost to him.

I told him to just stay down, to wait, I was going to come for him, except he couldn't hear me, couldn't see me.

He made it to his feet, swaying a little like he was having trouble balancing, then peeked through the tent flaps toward the sounds of men drinking and eating their fill by a fire.

"No, Tor. Don't. I'm coming. I promise, I'm going to save you." I sobbed, still on my knees, scrambling to get to him just as he moved like the wind out of the tent and ran.

He didn't make it far.

A Dramen with a gun hit him with its wooden handle on the head and Tor collapsed to the ground.

"Nooo!"

I woke up covered in sweat and the blankets thrown off the bed. My shoulders shook from the pain in my heart as I cried. My whimpers echoed around the stone walls. I was filled with the sense of being truly alone. Whether it was a nightmare or something else, it didn't matter. I knew Tor was with the Dramens and he suffered while I was here, serving wine and admiring pretty dresses while sipping tea with the queen.

My tears turned to anger. I was hurt by his omissions about who he was and that he was engaged. I was angry because he gave himself up so I could run here.

A scream of rage filled my lungs, as the tears kept coming. I wanted to thrash, to throw something, to punch something. Then it hit me. I remembered I was not completely alone. I could fight someone. I threw on some clothes I'd attempted to clean yesterday in the bathtub that were hanging dry on my wardrobe.

Rune might not even be up at this hour with the moon still shining through my window, but I needed to get out. I needed to make myself useful . . . do something . . . anything. I couldn't sit around while Tor suffered.

The halls were quiet. I grabbed a play wooden sword that had been set out for me to train with and stomped to the waterfall to practice.

Chapter Seventeen

I'd been outside for about an hour, practicing the sword positions Rune had shown me. Then I did the exercises Tor taught me to strengthen my body. I still lacked muscle tone. My physique was beginning to fill out since I ate real food consistently, but it wasn't enough.

Every tissue I built on was sore. I'd done everything to push each muscle group to the limit, pouring my anger and hopelessness into the movements. Just when I wanted to stop, I pictured Tor's battered body in the nightmare.

When the sun rose over the mountains to the east, I finally took my break on the bank of the river. Collapsing on my backside, I pooled water in my hands to drink. The chilled water was fresh, and my body needed it.

Once satisfied with being hydrated, I pulled off my shoes and stuck my sore feet in the cool water. My breathing was heavy, and I knew once Rune found me, it was only going to get worse. I welcomed that thought today. I wanted to train, I wanted to learn, and I wanted to pass out so deeply tonight that I wouldn't have another nightmare of Tor.

While listening to the water falling into the river, I missed what suddenly made rocks fall from the middle of the stone wall next to the falls. Jumping up quickly, I looked around for anything that had caused the stone to break in the one area. Nothing in sight. All the creatures Dris told me were in this land flashed through my mind. What if it was a werewolf, a dragon, or something dangerous?

I slowly backed away, realizing I shouldn't have come here alone at this hour. There was nothing here, and the rocks that had fallen were somewhere below the surface, too deep for me to examine. Not that I wanted to.

I saw movement behind the waterfall—something black. It looked like stones, but what if it wasn't? My stomach turned queasy, and my muscles tensed with adrenaline in case I needed to run or fight.

"What are you doing here?" A harsh voice bit into my scared state of mind.

Rune. I never thought there would be a day where I would be happy to see him. Beyond happy, I wrapped my arms around his muscular and clearly shocked body. I'd been so terrified in the moment of possibly being attacked by a creature, I turned from one enemy and ran into the arms of another. Once I realized what I did, I jumped back from a wide-eyed Rune.

"I'm sorry. I didn't mean to do that. There was just something here, and I was happy I wasn't alone." Heat warmed my cheeks with embarrassment.

Rune's eyes hardened, and his slacked jaw turned to granite beneath the light shadow of facial hair and skin. Without a word, he walked to the river with a hand steady on the hilt of his black sword.

"Something hit right there on the wall, and rocks fell. I didn't see it." I pointed to the jagged slice in the stones that wasn't there before. Rune huffed.

"It's gone now. Don't go in the woods at this hour without someone. You're an easy meal."

Instantly I regretted the vulnerability I'd let him see in me.

"I am an easy meal. I know I'm human. I know I can die easier than you. But I'm here, and I'm trying." I'd been throwing myself at this one hundred percent. "You know what?" I stood straighter, shifting my head to look off toward the waterfall instead of his unrelenting expression. I wanted to fight. I wanted to feel the pain. I wanted to take out my anger and frustrations. "Let's just train." Stomping over to where I left my shoes, I slipped them on and readied myself in a fighter's stance.

Rune's fingers quickly removed his sword belt and then removed the knives tucked into his boots. I wanted a fight, and Rune would give it to me without question.

Once the sharp weapons were safely in the grass, his massive frame lunged for me. I dove to the right fast, but not fast enough. His quick hand gripped my ankle and tugged. My body slammed to the ground hard. I didn't stay there for long, twisting my torso to block him from getting a better hold on my leg. I kicked and tried to get away, but he was smarter. I was pinned underneath his hard body seconds later.

My limbs thrashed and kicked. I used every ounce of strength I had to get out, only he remained strong and unyielding. A snarl ripped from my lungs in anger. He was proving to the little voice in my mind that it was right. I was useless. His icy stare focused on me as I fought with everything I had to create space between us, silently letting me exhaust myself.

It worked; I became tired. All the anger I'd had was gone, and now I felt like crap.

"You're not trying hard enough," he growled.

"I'm giving everything." My voice was louder, more like a scream.

"No. You're tired, and you're not thinking about what's at stake if you fail."

He thought I wasn't thinking about the stakes?

That did it.

With strength I didn't even know I was capable of and a movement I hadn't known to try, I lifted my hips at the same time I raised my arms above my head and tossed Rune over my body.

"You think I don't know what's at stake? Tor is with the Dramens! Your brother is being starved, tortured, and is on his way to the Iron City to be sold, bred, or killed. The man I love and care about is destined to die if I fail. I want to help the Fae. I want to help free Nyx, but I care about getting Tor away from those demons more than her. He's your brother. Don't you care about him?" I yelled and threw punches with each word. He dodged and blocked them, so I kept coming, shifting on my feet like I'd been doing this battle dance for ages instead of the few years of moderate practice.

"You know nothing about Tor or me." He spat blood that was coating his teeth to the grass.

He was bleeding. I stopped fighting instantly. I hadn't meant to hurt him; I didn't think I could. Lifting my hands to examine them, then his busted lip, I couldn't find any regret burning inside me that I'd caused his minor pain.

"I have to save him, Rune. I don't care if he is supposed to marry Nyx and ends up doing exactly that. I just want him safe."

"You think you'd be OK watching him marry someone else that isn't you? It's not as easy as you think." He spat more blood to the ground and touched the cut with his fingers. His scarred face shook with disbelief. He knew what it was like to love someone who was promised to another.

"I'll survive it like I've survived the fall of man." I would do whatever I had to do, even if it hurt my soul. I would figure it out as it happened.

"Now show me how to win in a fight against a Fae." I was done talking and fighting for the sake of rage. I wanted to push back the feelings of uselessness and learn something to help me toward my destiny to save Tor.

Chapter Eighteen

My mood hadn't improved the rest of the day. Rune handed my ass to me again and again. I ached and wanted to lay in bed for the rest of the day, except I had a job to do. Today I washed the crystals of the onyx tomb covering the princess. Since I had assumed this job was too important for me to do, I took the opportunity to get a good look at Nyx. The two guards at the door let me in and stood inside to watch me with my rag and bucket of water. Dust had settled over each pointed crystal.

About five minutes into scrubbing, I realized why I got the job. It wasn't because it was important. It was because this job sucked and they all outranked me. The crystals were sharp and hard to clean. Then you were practically staring at an unconscious woman the whole time, which would make anyone uncomfortable.

I'd asked the guards for some gloves so I wouldn't leave blood streaks on the crystal, and they didn't move or mutter one word. These silent Fae males were getting on my nerves. I couldn't get Rune to talk to me without being cruel, and these two were like toy soldiers standing their guard over a sleeping princess. The onyx was solid, and even when I threw my body weight into each scrub on the pointy crystals, it didn't move an inch.

How the hell was I supposed to free her?

I took a break from scrubbing and sat on the ground. I had to be patient. If I rushed after Tor or tried to break Nyx from this tomb right now, I would fail.

Breathe in. Breathe out. Breathe in. Breathe out. Mariam had taught me long ago how to calm myself when I was angry. Emotions had a way of taking over me when I didn't keep them in check, consuming my mind.

Instead of thinking about the bigger picture, I focused on the smaller pieces, breaking it down from saving the world to doing one thing at a time. Mariam had said one small act done each day became a large one over time. There was no difference in the end. Everything got done.

Taking one final deep breath, I'd found my mental bearings and stood. According to Tor, Princess Nyx had been placed in this tomb to protect her from the end. What happened at the end? The queen and king must have known—received some warning and hurried to protect their child. The more I thought about it, the more confused I became. The queen's core was diamond, and this was onyx.

Was the king's core made of onyx? I needed to learn more about Fae powers and how they correlated with their nature cores. I focused on the princess's sleeping form. She was beautiful, just like Tor had said: pearl skin, like her mother's; perfect, pink Cupid's-bow lips; high cheek bones; regal; and princess-like in every way. Her lavender tresses of hair flowed down gracefully on the altar she lay upon. A crown of purple, crystal flowers sat on her head, and her lilac-colored dress was decorative, yet elegant, showing off her woman's body.

Her delicate hands were placed over her abdomen as if she was dead. However, despite appearances she only rested in a state of waiting . . . waiting for me, if Celestine was to be believed. I searched around the tomb for any clues as to how I was supposed to save her, to undo what had been done.

There were not many details to go on from the woman before me. She looked like she had simply laid down and let them put her in there without a fight.

I wouldn't have done that, just let them hide me away while they all suffered or died. I would have fought for the people. But I also wasn't a princess who had a whole kingdom expecting me to protect it. There were many scenarios where I say I would act one way, and unless I was actually living it, there would be no real way to know how I'd respond.

A shimmer caught my eye from her torso. She wore four pieces of jewelry. First, a bracelet of turquoise blue gems set in small circles wrapped gently around her right wrist. Second, a simple brown ring with golden stripes was on her marriage finger. It was a simple band made out of an unfamiliar material, which was not gold or silver. Third, although her crown was exquisite, it was what I'd expect a princess like her to wear. Last, she wore a simple silver chain around her neck that ran down past the bodice of her dress to where her resting hands lay. She hid something beneath them, but I couldn't see beyond those delicate fingers.

My thirst to know more about the mystery object outweighed the desire to clean. I grabbed the rag and used it to protect my hands from getting sliced from the crystals, then started to climb. I briefly looked at the guards but neither of them said anything, although they watched me intensely. They knew I couldn't do anything to the princess, but if I impaled myself on one of these crystal spikes, they would have some explaining to do.

Reaching over, I took a step to the right and up one spike. I saw a small silver hoop attached to something dark, like a stone or a rock.

There had to be a better view than this.

The sun was hot and the crystals were heated as I tried to climb to the top, settling between two projections. The object was a blue, jagged, non-polished stone. I didn't know what it meant or if her jewelry was anything to obsess over. I did find it odd that a princess who was in a hurry to be set in this tomb looked completely at peace on the onyx-covered altar. Her hands gently rested over a blue stone the length of my middle finger like she had all the time in the world to get comfy before they encased her.

A cough from the guard echoed around the room, and I got the message: Get down and get back to my job of cleaning. Using the rag, I took one step at a time and my hands held onto the stone for balance. I heard the rip before my mind registered what the sound meant. Pain sliced into my hand, causing me to release my grip and I fell backward toward the ground. Another point of onyx sliced into my thigh on the way down.

I cursed and groaned in pain. Hot blood soaked my pants. I hoped the gash wasn't deep, but it still hurt like hell and was bleeding very badly. My head turned to the guards for help, but they hadn't moved an inch, their faces stoic. *Great.* Groaning, I twisted as best as I could toward the cleaning supplies to see if there was anything I could use to bandage the wounds. Beyond a bucket of water and a dirty torn rag, I had nothing.

I needed to get to my room or to a healer's place—somewhere I could clean the wounds, maybe stitch them up, and bandage them.

Gritting my teeth to hold back the pain-filled cry, I rose to my feet, trying to balance without touching my right foot to the ground. My bleeding left hand curled into my stomach, hoping the shirt would stop the blood from falling to the floor. No use in creating another mess I'd have to clean up once I was healed.

A mixture of hissing and hobbling became my rhythm on the way out of the room. The guards watched me, not moving, their focus darting back and forth between my wounds and the blood.

"I'll be back." I'd hoped my words sounded confident and less like a whimper. Sweat broke over my brow from the pain searing through me. They didn't stop me or call for assistance. They simply closed the door after I passed.

"Cold Fae," I cursed on a strangled breath.

My shirt was soaked from my hand, and my pant leg wasn't any better. The empty throne room was beginning to spin as I kept my limped walk toward my room.

"You're done. Good. They need you in the kitchen." Rune's voice echoed from behind me. As I spun to see his harsh face, the world slipped out from under me and I collapsed to the ground. The throne room and Rune turned to black.

Chapter Nineteen

"General, we are doing the best we can. She needed blood, which she has, and now she just needs time to rest." A sweet female voice rang through the darkness in my mind. My eyes fluttered open to see a wood ceiling above me. I blinked over and over, my eyelids feeling heavy. The desire to go back to sleep was tempting.

"I've seen wounds like that inflicted by Verin's swords, and the soldier was walking around an hour later," Rune growled, and if I my weak body could, I would have rolled my eyes.

"She's only human general, not Fae. If you're going to be a mother hen then you can go outside to your coop and wait for her. This is a healer's space, and your aggression doesn't help her heal any faster."

Whoever this woman was, I wanted to give her a high five. I didn't hear the door slam like I thought I would but heard a grunt and then a chair moving against the stone floor beneath us. My body didn't seem right. I tried turning my head to look at Rune and the healer, but nothing wanted to move.

"Are you fretting over me, Rune?" I meant to break the silence of the room with a joke. Mere seconds after I spoke, his blue-eyed face entered my line of sight with the blond-haired healer pushing him out of her way. She had a sweet face. Her pointed ears and canines gave her away as Fae, if her aging beauty didn't signal her heritage first.

"How are you feeling, dear?" she asked, her hands moving to touch my forehead, then my cheek softly.

"I can't really feel much. Am I paralyzed?" My stomach clenched at the thought. Hopefully that meant I was OK.

"No, you will be able to move in another thirty minutes. I gave you an herb to numb the pain while I fixed you up. The crystal that cut your thigh hit an artery. But all is fixed and you just need to rest. I'll have a salve for you to put on the wounds to help with healing and any scar tissue." She lifted my cut hand into my view. It was stitched up and clean with a green paste over it. I assumed it was something to ward off infection.

"If he bothers you, feel free to kick him out." She winked at me, then left my view.

Rune was there in an instant, his scarred face a sight for sore eyes.

"Why were you climbing on the onyx?" he asked, his tone rushed, like he'd been waiting to ask me for hours.

"To look at something." I wasn't sure if what I saw was worth mentioning or not. I'd barely had time to think about it before I fell.

"Don't do that again." His words weren't harsh, like he was watching his tone with me. He almost appeared concerned, for once.

"I won't," I promised, and it was the truth. I had no interest at all climbing to my potential death again.

"How did I get here?" I asked, while attempting to look around for anything familiar.

"I carried you," he stated, which caught me off guard.

"I figured you would have let me bleed out than carry me anywhere." I tried to laugh, but my mouth was dry.

"I can't let you die." His jaw twitched from clenching.

Of course he couldn't let me die. I was the chosen one to save his love, and I hoped he cared enough about Tor to want me alive to rescue him, too.

"Right." He didn't need to go into any more detail about his reasons for making sure I was still breathing. It hung in the air between us like a heavy fog. My eyes closed as the fatigue set in.

"I don't hate you."

My eyelids flew open immediately and settled on his unreadable expression.

"What?" I needed him to say it again. His response was comical. His eyes rolled and he smirked. It was almost like he was being playful . . . so uncharacteristic for him.

"I must be dead . . . still impaled on an onyx tomb. You just rolled your eyes. The Rune I know would do no such thing," I teased, and he just shook his head at my ridiculousness.

"I don't hate you, Sapphira."

My name. He said my name.

His harsh face softened, and for a moment I didn't feel like his enemy number one.

"You just remind me of her. It makes me on edge." The weight of his honesty crushed my chest like he'd sat a mighty boulder on me. His remorse was visible, his breaths full of heavy burdens.

I reminded him of her. The princess.

I cleared my throat. A ball of nerves settled in my belly as I dared to ask my thoughts. "Will you tell me about her?" I wanted to know so many things about her, but he might not be comfortable talking about her to me.

"Another time."

This interaction was unsettling, even after he was called away but promised to return to help me to my room. We hadn't fought. Maybe becoming friends was in the realm of reality and not a fantasy after all. The longer I sat on the healer's bed, I thought about what I had discovered, and the more I concluded I couldn't do this on my own. I needed to know everything, and I needed help.

Rista, the wonderful and attentive healer, gave me the OK to head back to my room with instructions on how to use the salve in the tin she gave me. Rune appeared as soon as I stood from the bed. The weight on my leg ached in my thigh and shot a tinge of lightning-hot pain up my spine. The normally prickly Rune caught me as I lost my balance. His strong Fae arms scooped me up with no hesitation.

"Don't jostle her too much, General," Rista warned, then held the door open for us to go through. Rune carried me like a babe against his chest into the moonlit gardens. The healer's quarters were just outside the palace. I didn't blame her for wanting to be away from the commotion that happened within the royal stone walls. The quiet ambiance made for better healing.

"You don't have to carry me. She said I could walk." I peered up at his face, expecting him to dump me in the grass. But he didn't, and I felt just as awkward as I had when he was being kind to me earlier. Unsure of where I was supposed to put my hands, I rested them against my chest. Clinging to him would have brought things between us to a different level . . . a level I wasn't sure I wanted to cross.

He held me like I was nothing but a feather in his arms, one hand beneath my knees and the other holding my back against him. Instinctively, I breathed in his scent with every breath and found him oddly soothing. He smelled like the waterfall where we had spent time training—crisp, clean, and with a pinch of sandalwood, like he bathed in the cool waters every night.

"You smell nice," I mumbled as the fatigue from the day overcame me. At least that was my excuse, but I felt safe, resting in his arms, the same feeling I had with Tor lying next to me every night.

I didn't hear if he stayed silent or grunted. Exhaustion won as we passed through the palace doors.

Chapter Twenty

I managed to clean and dress myself without much trouble in the morning. Rune had brought my sleeping body to my quarters and covered me in the blanket thrown over my small bed.

My mind was too distracted by the racing thoughts of yesterday's interaction with him to jump when the pounding on my door began. My limp was noticeable but with the salve Rista gave me, there wasn't much pain in the movement.

Rune waited for me, his expression as frosty as the mountain peaks once again. My shoulders tensed in defense, ready for the old Rune to return.

"You're going to the library, then taking the afternoon off." His words were flat, but he didn't appear aggravated.

"Thank you. Are we uh . . . friends?" I probably shouldn't have been so blunt. Only I wanted to know if I should guard myself around him or if I could speak more freely . . . maybe even talk to him about Nyx.

He pondered on the word "friends," not answering me right away. My fingers twitched to slam the door and curl up in bed, hiding from the embarrassing assumption that things had changed between us.

"I don't have many friends. Most people are afraid of me," he admitted, making me want to press him for more information about himself. Sure, his personality was like a bush of thorns, but he wouldn't carry me around tenderly or care for me physically if he was pure evil. Even in her mental state, the queen wouldn't have him as the general of her armies if he was no better than Verin.

Was it his scars that spoke some Fae language that I couldn't understand? Had his love for Nyx caused tension between the people? I wanted to know.

"Then consider yourself with one more friend. I know I'm a simple human, but I've got charisma," I joked, smiling at him like I hadn't before. He studied my upturned lips like they were a weapon pointed at him instead of a simple grin. He didn't speak, and I decided that was enough for me. I limped over to my shoes to slip them on gently and made my way back to Rune.

"Now that we are friends instead of enemies, feel free to divulge all your inner secrets to me. I'll even let you in for a sleepover where I can braid your black hairs and have a pillow fight." I'd seen another side of the general and there was no going back. I was going to joke with him. Maybe Dris was right. Prickly on the outside but the inside? Not so much.

He scoffed at my attempt to lighten his mood and walked toward the library. I wasn't sure if he realized it or did it on purpose, but his gait lacked its normal long stride, and his steps weren't as hurried. He was slowing himself for me and my injured leg. Turns out a close call with death was all it took to turn Rune from a beast into a man.

Dris waited for me in front of the magnificent library. There were no goodbyes or glances exchanged as Rune walked off and left me with the excited librarian.

Today her hair was a crazy mess of white waves on her head. Her dress was a pale green that ended above her knees, and she was barefoot.

"I'm so glad you're OK. I heard about what happened, and I was so worried about you. You seem like you have healed for the most part." She rushed to my side and gave me her arm in case I needed the extra help to walk. I didn't but accepted her gesture anyway. It was nice having someone genuinely want to be helpful for nothing in return.

"Thanks, I'm OK. It smarts a bit but the salve Rista gave me really helps. I'm glad today is a calmer day."

The thoughts of training didn't sound like fun at all today, maybe not even tomorrow. I wasn't sure Rune would call that off, though. There was probably some form of battle he could teach me in my current state. No day was to be wasted when his princess and Tor's life was on the line.

"Wonderful! I've got a bunch of stuff planned for us today on the table. Did you have anything particular you were curious about? I love questions." Her gentle features made me feel like I could trust her and tell her everything, maybe even consider her a friend, if we got to know each other more.

"I do have some questions."

She helped me sit in the wooden chair that I'd been in last time at the same table. There wasn't anyone in the library again, which made me think it wasn't a place people came as often as Dris would like them to. All these books were a good thing to have around. Knowledge could be a useful weapon in the upcoming weeks.

She sat in the seat across from me and waited patiently. "OK, shoot. What are your questions?" She viewed this as a game, testing her skills and intelligence.

"Right. I have a few. Is there a catalog somewhere of nature cores in people? Like who has what inside them? And how does it all work with and without magic?"

I didn't ask who had an onyx core flowing through their body since I was unsure how nature cores in the Fae worked. Was the queen's heart made up of a diamond or something?

Dris's eyes sparkled with delight over my thoughtful questions. She leaped into action and went to a bookshelf to the right, then the left. The two books she grabbed were perfectly lined and organized next to each other on the table once she returned.

"There is a book of such things, although it is a tad out of date. We try our best to keep records of births and deaths, but without magic, it has become a little harder. Are you looking for anyone or a core in particular?" She opened a large book that was dusty in the cracks of the leather binding the side. It had a symbol on the front—Crysia's symbol—with the crystal tree and its roots growing into a sword pointing up. The Fae loved their intricate details, and it was mesmerizing.

"Just kind of everyone. I don't know many gem names, and I would like to learn about the families." I didn't know many names of the precious stones, so this would help me learn about them, while finding out who onyx belonged to.

"And for your other question. I want you to close your eyes."

I did as she commanded in her sweet tone. My other senses woke up to take over the loss of sight. The library smelled like lemon from the cleaning soap we used to wipe down the floors and the furniture. The sound of the waterfall could be heard in the distance with birds chirping nearby.

"Think of your heart, pumping inside your chest. We Fae have a heart like yours and inside that heart lies our cores, our very essence. Like a light if you will, shining inside us. Mine is a snowy owl core. It's common in my family tree. Back when magic was alive and prospering, I was able to transform into an owl. It was beautiful flying high over the trees. I still feel it, coursing through my veins, filling me, but I can't change anymore. None of the Fae who were in their human forms twenty years ago can. Some are still trapped in their animal forms." Her voice tapered off. That chest guarding my heart ached for her, for the Fae.

She took a breath and continued on, pushing past the pain that weighed heavily on her. "Now depending on the strength of the Fae, and their core or cores . . . yes, I see those wide eyes. There are a very strong few who have two cores. Genetics and fate decide that. There is no way to choose who gets what. Certain cores may stay in the family, but that isn't always the case." She gave me a mischievous smile. She enjoyed shocking me with this information. I enjoyed hearing about this world, even though what she was saying was beyond my imagination.

"Back to what I was saying. Depending on the cores and the strength of the Fae, even without their powers or magic, the essence of the core is still inside them. Every life in the world has a vibration, an energy that it creates. And if the core is more toward the animal side, then we take on a similar personality to that of the beasts inside us. Owls are intelligent. They are sharp and keen of sight. They are also suspicious creatures, always watching, looking for danger or prey around them. Same with the gem cores. All gems have certain properties and purposes. Diamonds are the strongest gem in the world. Queen Olyndria is the only person in our history to have been given a diamond core. She is the most powerful in our existence and has lived a long time. Diamonds are known for being the stone of invincibility. They are energy amplifiers and symbols of love and purity. Sometimes when the queen isn't feeling herself, those around her can feel her emotions, and their own are heightened. It's a problem only strong Fae have when someone is close enough to touch them. You feel the vibrations and energy from their cores."

So much information. My head ached from all the details. Then the keen-of-sight, intuitive owl Fae called me out.

"Now for the question you really wanted to ask. Who has an onyx core?"

Chapter Twenty-One

No one.

The answer was no one.

I thought it was odd because Tor had told me the king and queen put the princess in her onyx tomb. But according to Dris, the king did not have a core of onyx, and only the host of the core could create the crystals. A diamond core couldn't create a ruby, only diamonds. That's why the symbol of Crysia, the tree in the throne room had diamond leaves. Olyndria was its creator.

"Why hadn't anyone noticed that or said anything?"

"When everything happened, the people were too panicked to think about it. Our king's stone is obsidian. Looks sort of similar, enough that no one questioned what happened. No one likes to read the history of King Lachan, either. He lived a boring life until he courted and married the queen. Even now he is off on a hunt, while the queen takes care of the kingdom."

I thought about all I'd learned as I sat in the garden after my lesson with Dris, watching creatures whose name I didn't know run around chasing each other. They looked like squirrels, but they were a bluish-purple color with black eyes, which would have been frightening if it weren't for their large pointed ears and cute actions. One would steal a red berry from the other, then they would chase each other around and the thief would give it back before taking it again and playing the game all over again. I giggled more in that moment watching those two go back and forth than I had in weeks.

My fingers lightly caressed the symbol of Crysia on the birth records book Dris told me to take, as well as the list of nature cores known to their world. After this short moment of rest in the gardens, I'd head back to my quarters and read.

There was this relentless yearning inside me that craved the knowledge in these two books like a drug, and I was eager to satisfy the appetite. Anything to help me gain the upper hand with this epic destiny I'd been thrown into. Dris said she would search every book she had for the answer to who had an onyx core. It wasn't in the books I held in my hands. I wondered if someone altered the fact to keep the truth from being discovered.

The queen would be an obvious choice to ask, but she couldn't exactly give me a name or tell me the long and complicated story if there was one. She couldn't string words together that I understood, let alone give away secrets to the kingdom.

No, I still had time, and I could figure this out.

Dris was on my team. Now I needed to get a broody warrior to sit down and have a chat with me. He could fill in details about the princess and what happened. I doubt that if his love was being encased in onyx, he would let it happen if he was nearby. He knew things . . . things I needed to know.

Getting Rune to open up was going to take time . . . and trust. "In time," I told myself, trying to project the best in this complicated situation.

I wanted a real day off to walk around Crysia and see the shops and the people. I wanted to stroll in the woods, watching the creatures that lingered there. My thoughts flashed back to the noise at the waterfall yesterday. Maybe having someone go into the woods with me would be a better decision than trying to go alone. Danger could be lurking to eat me in one solid gulp there.

The sun was high, and my stomach growled. It was getting used to this eating-on-command thing and was making up for lost time. Jostling the books against my chest, I stood awkwardly and limped toward the kitchen for the bread I had smelled earlier. Another ball would be happening tonight. The Fae loved to party. The kitchen was busy, and I barely managed to grab some fruit and bread before being nudged out of the way.

Tonight, I had more important things to do, so I didn't even bother offering to play wine girl. The head servant would have run me ragged, anyway, and my leg needed rest.

It was odd not having an escort walk me around, but I assumed they knew by now I wasn't going to do anything, or maybe Celestine had spoken up about my little freedom. Whatever the reason, I was grateful to walk where I pleased in the palace.

The belt around my waist was the first to go after setting my plate next to the bed. I attempted to get cozy for my date with these books. Once my pants were off, the long-sleeved dress that cut at my hips and became a point by my knees was my only attire. My thighs and legs were on display but no one was going to see them, and this would make putting Rista's salve on my leg easier.

The fire danced in the hearth, keeping my small room warm, and I had extra pieces of wood ready to throw in when it started to dwindle. The bread and fruit appeased my stomach after I'd taken my time to savor every bite, while enjoying the view out the window. I saw people walking around the city's cobblestone roads. The market was busy, and kids played in a field nearby. It looked heavenly, and as much as I wanted to be like the Fae, going to the ball in their fancy dresses, I'd rather spend my time with the common folk, sampling the various foods from the market below and meeting the artists and vendors who stood by their merchandise. One day I would get to visit that part of the kingdom, and I would live out my fantasy of experiencing all this kingdom had to offer.

I settled in my bed, my back against the stone wall. I placed the records book on my lap and the nature book to my left. That way I'd be able to go back and forth and examine the name of each core and its innate energy.

"Let's see who the oldest Fae is." I lifted the cover and flipped to the first page of Crysia's birth records.

Celestine's family was at the top of the list. Her grandmother, Magrithia, with a moonstone core, continued to breath the glorious air for the past 5,522 years. According to Tor's stories, Fae were immortal, but it still shocked me to see the numbers written down collectively.

Chapter Twenty-Two

The moon was high, and the Fae below danced like morning would not approach their party.

The Fae continued to fascinate me with their nature cores. There were owl, rabbit, lion, elephant, rose, and oak tree cores inside a Fae's living essence. Every person had the personality of each core inside them, along with powers had magic remained. Around 900 years ago, there was even a dragon core to a man in a neighboring kingdom. According to the book, the man was deceased and had no relatives. Wouldn't it have been cool to meet someone who had the essence of a dragon inside him?

Tor's family had either gems or a wolf line inside them, with a rare person chosen every few centuries to have the essence of a werewolf. The nature core's book explained it was indeed very rare, but could travel down bloodlines, as with a dragon core.

The gem cores were my favorite. There were so many kinds, along with their different energies. The queen's diamond was the strongest, and no other diamond had been born inside another Fae. Other kingdoms had rubies or emeralds but not diamond. King Lachan had an obsidian core . . . powerful but nothing like his queen. She knew no equal power in this realm. However, I believed in balance, and everything had an energy that needed an opposite or a match to keep the world moving.

I wished I could have found out Tor's history from him personally, but I had to look at his name in the book. Torin Wolfstrom, age fifty-three, nature core turquoise. It fit the man I had come to know. He always radiated truth and protection. He grounded me in ways that made me feel safe. All of that was part of his essence in his core, his very blood. Turquoise was a protection stone, the definition of Tor. Despite being significantly older than me, he still looked young. I thought about the lies and omissions he made to keep his identity from me. *Why didn't he tell me the truth?*

I forced myself to move on from the sting of his secrets. I loved him, and I could forgive him once he was safe. Since his brother's details were right above his, I read about Rune's core. Surely it had to be a rotten apple, except what I found was shocking. Rune, 202 years old, had two cores, a rare occurrence even Tor and the queen did not possess.

A tiger's eye gem marked him as a royal like his brother, its essence rooted in strength, patience, and determination, which fit the general perfectly. Everything Rune emitted and showed in his personality came from that core . . . patience to wait for a love encased in onyx for twenty years, loyal and hopelessly waiting against all odds. The strength of that wait alone was hard to imagine, but in the week I'd known him, it fit him perfectly. He was a protector and true to those he cared about. Nothing would stop him from getting what he wanted.

Rune had both gem and wolf cores, but not just any wolf . . . a werewolf core.

Dots lined up in my head. I wondered if he scarred himself while becoming a werewolf. His personality was prickly and feral. People usually gave him a wide berth, and he wasn't very welcoming. They knew what he was and feared him, not only as a skilled warrior but because of his rare werewolf core.

I wondered if I asked him about his dual cores, if he would answer me honestly. Then I laughed thinking of the answer. He'd probably say no and tell me to do more arm exercises.

Princess Nyx had an amethyst core. Her hair and body matched the coloring of the purple gem. Some Fae took after their cores in appearance. She displayed the amethyst's properties of peace, stability, and calmness. Maybe I needed to go around her tomb when Rune pissed me off. Then my thoughts drifted toward the onyx.

No one in the book had an onyx core, which continued to befuddle me. Who helped the queen protect the princess if it wasn't the king? His core was black, but there were subtle differences. Obsidian was like volcanic glass; onyx was a simple gem. Its energy was protection, quieting, and strength. If I hadn't just read that Rune's gem core was a tiger's eye, I would have leaned toward his core being onyx. It made sense that he would be the one to work with the queen to protect his love. However, if it was his strength, then he would be able to reverse what was done.

Magic wasn't in this realm anymore. No one—not even the powerful queen—could reverse it because they couldn't use their nature cores. The Fae were like mortals except for being long-lived.

I closed the books quickly, my mind not able to handle any more information. I set them on the table and stared at the Fae dancing in the garden below. Over and over I churned the idea of how I could possibly get the princess out of the tomb without magic. What talents did I possess for this seemingly impossible task?

There was still so much I didn't know, so much to ferret out, and there was only one person to give me some insight. I was too wired to sleep, too invested in this overwhelming mystery. I had to talk about my finding and sort out my thoughts.

Throwing on my slippers, I peered into the hall to make sure no one was there before slipping from my room and making my way toward Celestine's cave. Hopefully, since she had been a seer, she would know I was coming. I'd hate to wake her but I was too hyped over everything I'd learned. I needed to know more, and she was my answer.

I passed three guards on the way out, none of them moving from their posts. They only watched me. As I walked onto the grass, a brisk wind fluttered my tunic and the chill bore into my bones.

Shit. I was so determined to get out of the room and find Celestine that I forgot to grab some pants. While the thought was embarrassing that the guards had seen my bare legs, I didn't turn around to change. My attire was still more modest than some of the Fae dresses at the ball tonight.

"Sapphira." The cave winds whispered to me again. This time I didn't shy away or crave to run. I took a step without faltering into the stone narrows toward the only person who could answer my questions.

Chapter Twenty-Three

Celestine waited for me by her cat-owl creatures. The first time I arrived, the sight had shocked me, but now I was more familiar with the Fae realm and its inhabitants. I wasn't shocked when I saw some tea and grapes on a plate waiting for me on the ground by the fire.

"You do know everything, huh?" I joked, while plopping down where I was supposed to, making sure my dress wasn't showing anything I didn't want seen.

"I've only seen as far as I dared look before the magic was gone, which was thousands of years. I have some ways to go before I am surprised, my dear." She enjoyed my light teasing.

"Then you know why I'm here."

Her pointed fingers smoothed over the head of a white owl cat; its purr quietly echoed around the dark woods.

"I do, and you must know I can't tell you everything." She continued stroking the happy creature.

"I don't understand why. If you want me to save the princess, then tell me how." Maybe it was cheating to know the future, but I was out of my league with this place and this destiny.

Celestine pondered my words, remaining silent as she pet her friend a few more times before strolling over without making a sound. Graciously, she lowered her body, her cape drifting out of her way to across from me and the fire.

"Do you not think the future would change if I told you what was to come? Are you ready for the answers you seek?" She tilted her head to the side with interest.

If she was to tell me I would have to die in order to open the tomb, would I go through with it? Or if I was going to lose someone like the queen or Dris, could I sacrifice them?

"The destination is not what matters in a hero's story, only how he or she got there. When all hope seems lost, the hero battles on, refusing to give up. You have it in you. You feel it in your very blood that you can do this. You're just impatient."

I wanted to stomp my feet and argue like a child because I knew she was right. I had only been in this realm for a week. I still had three more until I would rescue Tor. What else would occur between now and then?

"I'm afraid." Confessing my fear aloud wasn't easy. Better telling her than it slipping out around Rune.

"Fear is in your head; the danger is what's real. Fear is your mind telling you to run, and if you run, you'll never know what it's like to live, my dear. To face the danger and leave the fear behind is a true hero's destination."

It was like being hit with a hammer in the chest. She was right—completely. From the nerves firing in my mind to the tips of my toes, her words seeped into my very being.

"I hope I can live up to this amazing person in your head."

"That's up to you. Who you want to be entirely depends on the decisions you make. You can choose to leave the survivor side of you back in the community where the rest of your former people died and become the warrior you were always meant to be. Or you can stay as you are, a survivor of the apocalypse and nothing more."

I was speechless. It was a lot to live up to being someone I didn't believe I could be. But that was part of the problem. I didn't believe. I was letting the fear and possibility of failing hold me back. I snatched a few of the grapes and sipped some tea. Every thought I'd come in here with had silenced.

"Now that my grand speeches have been made, I can give you a few little details that won't cause any harm to the future." She leaned in, her hands rubbing against each other like she was gearing up to do something like magic.

I set the cup down and gave her my complete attention. If she was willing to part with information, then I would take every word into memory like it was life or death because in the end it might be.

"I know you read about Rune and his cores. Do not be afraid of him. He will not hurt you. Don't approach him about them; he will tell you in his own time. Heed my warning." I would keep my mouth sealed despite wanting to ask him questions. If I bombarded him with my thoughts before trust between us grew, he would completely shut down.

"Anything else?" I dared to ask. There had to be more morsels of the future for me to gobble up.

"You can trust Dris. She will be a very helpful friend to you in times to come."

She smiled, her white teeth beaming in the moonlight. Her cat-owl hooted, which still sounded like a meow.

"In two days' time, your general will be away. I suggest a nice long walk in the Hallowstag Woods while he is gone. A creature of legend will find you. Do not be afraid when he shows himself."

Her mischievous smile blatantly indicated there was something more to her words. I wanted to know what she hid from me, but if I knew, would I still go for a walk in the woods?

"One last matter before you go back to the palace. Pay attention to your dreams, dear, for in them we see things our conscious minds did not. Answers to your own questions might be in your head, waiting for you to acknowledge them."

She stood there with her creatures one minute, and then was gone, like smoke billowing from the fire.

Her departure surprised me, but I'd give her points for intrigue. I sat by the fire, eating and drinking. The tea she gave me was most likely some concoction to help me relax. She liked me calm, and I did, too. My mind reeled from everything she said. It was all so grand, even though none of my questions were answered. I didn't know who had an onyx core or how I was going to save the princess and Tor. I did feel different as I gathered my strength to stand and leave for the palace—stronger, like I had been given the right kind of pat on the back needed to push through.

Rune stood by the cave's exit when I walked out into the chilled night's air. "The guards told me you were out taking a midnight stroll." His arms were crossed over his broad chest; his stance told me he was not fond of me being here and having to come fetch me.

I wondered how long he'd been out here waiting for me, and why he hadn't come in and demanded I leave at once. "I needed some answers." I kept walking and he fell in line beside me, his large body protecting me from the chilly wind.

"Did you get any of use?" His curious tone replaced his usual disgruntled voice. I shook my head no.

"However, I did learn something that I think will be helpful. We still have a few more weeks. I'll figure it out in the end."

Hope blossomed in my chest. I needed to believe in myself more than I ever had before. I needed to do as Celestine said and let Sapphira, the survivor of the apocalypse, lay with the rest of mankind and become someone else. The Sapphira I was meant to be.

Maybe I'd fail. I was scared of that failure, the shame of not living up to this great person in everyone's heads. If I failed, people died, so I had to keep going, even with the fear grasping my heart.

Rune stayed quiet as we walked back through the palace's arched doors, the sounds of the ball reverberating through the air with laughter and music. I wanted to dance and sway along with the notes as they traveled through the halls.

"Do you dance, Rune?" The words were out before I could stop them.

His eyebrows lifted, his face taking on a younger appearance. I'd surprised the great, cranky General Rune, an accomplishment fit for a medal.

"I can." Maybe the princess was his only dancing partner, a position he wouldn't give to anyone else.

"I bet you could sway like the best of them, shake those Fae hips and drive the ladies wild," I teased, enjoying myself. I giggled, feeling lighter than I had when I had left the palace earlier.

Once we arrived at my door, I expressed my gratitude, and I wasn't sure who was more surprised. "I know I'm probably a pain in the ass but thank you for being there, making sure I don't get eaten by the creatures that go bump in the night."

While he may have ulterior motives behind escorting me to places or making sure I didn't die, I still appreciated it.

"You shouldn't dress like that outside your room," he said, noting my outfit and the bare brown skin on display.

"Nothing compared to the Fae ladies I see around here. Plus, I'm only human. No one is going to stoop low enough to gaze at my mortal body."

I was absolutely OK with it. I had a boyfriend. Well ... sort of.

His gaze hardened once more, and his relaxing posture stood tall and rigid. Conversation was over. He had filled his quota for the day and needed to recharge his social batteries for tomorrow where he might need to speak to someone. "Goodnight Rune." I opened the door and gave him one last glance before heading inside. His eyes were on my legs like they were poisonous snakes. I couldn't help it. I raised my leg at him like it was going to bite. The slit on the front of my thigh rose higher, exposing more skin, which seemed to cause him more displeasure. He walked away and I laughed to myself, closing the door behind me.

Still giggling, I snuggled into the bed, leaving my slippers strewn about on the floor.

Chapter Twenty-Four

"An answer for a hit target?" I must not have heard him right as I stared into his not-so-angry face. Unease drifted over me at the hint of a smile growing on his pink lips.

"You hit the target, I'll answer one of your questions." He confirmed what I heard, but it still seemed suspicious. I crossed my arms over my chest, wary of what seemed to be happening here.

"What's the trick?" Rune had escorted me to a training court I hadn't seen beside the palace. Men and women warriors practiced their skills in hand-to-hand combat and weaponry. It was the place where blood and sweat appeared to be required to stay. He'd walked to a small armory and grabbed a bow and quiver of arrows, then we strolled to the waterfall shore, his preferred training area.

It wasn't a compound bow like I'd used before but a wood-carved traditional-type, lighter despite being made out of wood. Hopefully I wouldn't have much difficulty operating this kind.

"No trick. I think I'm figuring you out." He shrugged as if this wasn't a big deal to him. I looked around one more time. No one else was here.

OK then.

I lifted the bow, testing the pull of the string briefly. The target was ten yards away, a round piece of wood, maybe a lid to a wine barrel with a sheet over it and a dot in the middle. I was a decent shooter, and I did have questions for Rune. With the motivation of Rune opening up to me, I grabbed an arrow and nocked it against the string and the riser of the bow. Pulling back the arrow, placing the feathers against the side of my lips, I took a deep breath in, filled my lungs, lined up my shot toward the little black dot, and released with my exhaled breath. It flew straight and then missed.

"Son of a—" I stopped myself from cursing too loudly so I wouldn't frighten any slumbering creatures nearby. Rune looked at the target and then back at me, his face impassive.

"Again."

Yeah again. I made better shots than that one back home. Mariam had taught me the basics and Tor had continued with the education. While I wasn't the worst at the bow, I was much better with a sword. My weapons' expertise was not high since only the small regiment at the community had them. Not much good it did them against the Dramens, though. This time I would hit the target. I nocked my arrow again and raised it with confidence. Holding in my belly, lifting my chest, and breathing in, believing the arrow would fly true. It didn't.

Without Rune even telling me to try again, I grabbed more arrows and shot them in rapid fire. If taking my time wasn't working, then the power of probability was bound to kick in. One was statistically going to hit the target eventually and save me from the embarrassment of being a poor shot.

"Finally!" I shouted, lifting the bow and my hands in the air in victory, my ninth arrow barely touching the black dot.

"It still counts!" I looked at Rune while he examined it.

"You're a poor shot, but I'll let you have this one." He waited expectantly, his hands on his hips.

I'd been so focused on shooting, I hadn't decided which of my many questions would be first.

"How old are you?"

His black scarred eyebrow raised. "You had the chance to ask me anything and that's the first question you go with?"

I nodded. Even though I knew the answer, he didn't know I did. "I'm testing the waters to see if you will tell me the truth or not."

"I never lie."

I believed he spoke the truth. Despite knowing the answer before he muttered the words, I wanted to have that faith in his honesty validated. I grabbed another arrow and tapped it against my good leg expectantly. He rolled his eyes, then answered my question.

"Two hundred and two."

My next arrow hit the black dot right in the middle. Maybe all I needed was to warm up my aim.

"How did you meet the princess?" I was curious about their story. I wondered if she had returned his feelings, and what their life was like before everything fell. How did it all tie together with Tor?

Rune didn't balk or grimace at my question. He was a smart Fae. He knew I was going to ask questions about her. When I was injured, he had said he'd tell me another time. Today was another time.

"I was coming to meet the queen and king before Torin arrived to accept the betrothal to Nyx. She was covered in a hood and fighting off three goblins in the Hallowstags by herself. I assisted her but didn't know who she was until later that night."

It sounded romantic, the way he came in like some white knight. I bet she loved it. I said it out loud and he roared with laughter. I couldn't lift another arrow to the bow or shoot the target for another answer. Rune, the Fae I'd never seen fully smile or jest, was laughing. It was one of the most beautiful sights I'd ever seen in my life.

"She was pissed, actually, having gone out in search of trouble on purpose. I have a tiny scar on my right shoulder from when she poked her sword into my arm for me to back away and let her finish battling alone."

My kind of woman, and the way she handled Rune? No wonder he was in love with her. She stood up to the big bad wolf.

"Did she love you in return?" Once again, my mouth had run with my thoughts without a consultation with my mind. The lightness I'd seen in him moments before was gone. Sadness and longing had returned with his tensed muscles.

"Fifteen yards. Hit your target and I'll answer."

It wasn't a no; he would answer a question I had thought about so many times as long as I hit the target from farther away.

At first, I beamed confidence. Then failed attempt after failed attempt shoved that confidence somewhere I couldn't reach. When our training came to an end, I tried to help Rune carry the target, but he snapped to leave it. He picked up a larger bow and set of arrows he'd left by a tree nearby and stood in position to shoot.

"We were mates, and she loved me fiercely. Enough to go against everything."

He shot the target into the little black dot, splitting my arrow in two.

Chapter Twenty-Five

"What did you figure out? A little bird told me you sneaked out in your night garments to see my aunt." Dris sat next to me this time instead of across the book-covered table. Her features beamed with interest for the information I'd ferreted out. Celestine said to trust her, and I really needed a friend, someone else to talk to besides Rune and that one time with the queen.

"Lots of things, and yet, not a lot." Two Fae at the next table looked over at the selection of books to our left.

"Are we safe to talk here?" I whispered, even though I'm sure if those Fae were paying attention, they would have heard me.

She shook her head, then grabbed my hand to pull me up with her. Her hand was soft, like feathers caressing my skin gently. I liked the sensation of someone else touching me. I'd been without a hug or a gentle squeeze of my fingers, and I hadn't realized how much those simple gestures meant to me.

I didn't feel so lonely.

Dris walked us from the table of books to a door on the back wall. A silver key in her hand unclicked the lock with ease. It was only wide enough for one person to walk through at a time, but when my eyes adjusted to the dimmer light, I saw another smaller library with only about ten dark wooden shelves. Spider webs dangled between each like a warning to stay away. Dust was thick in the air, and the only light in the room was from a stained-glass window to the right. There were no art decorations, yet the room held a sense of beauty.

"This is the dark library. Only me, the queen, and her advisor are allowed in here. I believe that you are meant to be in here, as well. No one can hear what we speak of, and there are books that might aid your quest." We walked to the only table in the room, which had two dusty chairs. My hands were dirty from wiping the thick layer of dust before we sat down.

"OK, give me the details." She sat next to me, her hands in her lap. Her body practically hummed with eagerness for new information.

"Celestine didn't give me much, and I get it. I have to live the journey if I am going to get to where I'm supposed to go."

Dris nodded.

"Did you know about Rune and Nyx?" I needed to talk to someone about it, and I hoped I wasn't betraying Rune somehow by discussing it with her.

"I knew. Some others did, too. But she was promised to be with Prince Torin." Her sigh echoed in the quiet room. The whole thing between the three of them was sounding more and more tragic every time I heard about it.

"Rune said they were mates. Does that mean what I think it means?" I sucked in a breath, my body frozen as I waited to hear if something so indefinite existed.

Her hands covered her mouth as she gasped. "He said they were mates?" she asked, and again, I nodded.

"Finding your mate is not rare. It does happen frequently between Fae. But it is an eternal bonding, sacred and cherished. Some never find their mates and are happy that way. Some Fae spend eternity searching for theirs. Just as nature decides our internal cores, it also selects a pair when we are created. A match and a balance to ourselves."

Nyx was Rune's match . . . his mate.

"I never knew that they were . . ." She couldn't finish her sentence, like the thought shook her thoroughly or perhaps filled her with too much sorrow to say the words aloud.

"He loves her a lot. It's why he's helping me because he believes I can save her. I don't think he cares much for the fact that I am supposed to save Tor, too."

"They were quite a pair together, the princess and Rune. Truly a case of opposites attracting, to say the least. They really did try not to fall for each other and fought to keep their growing interest a secret while Tor courted her, but now knowing they were mates, they really didn't have a choice in the matter."

Poor Tor. Poor Rune.

"Did Tor love her?" I kept my voice even, wanting to hear more of their history, although it might be painful.

Dris's expression filled with understanding and support. "I know he was enamored by her. As were many men, but something always gave me the impression he was only doing it because he was pressured into it. She was beautiful, so it wasn't a hard decision for him to make. They did not look at each other the same way Rune and Nyx did when they thought no one was watching them. We owls knew, though. We see everything." She held her body straight and confident, proud of herself and her heritage. I hoped she was right. If I managed to accomplish all that was set at my feet, Tor and Nyx could be reunited, and I might have to let him go if she chose him.

Needing to change the subject to something less soul crushing, I explained what Celestine said about meeting a creature in the woods. Dris warned me about the creatures in the Hallowstags, so I promised to take a weapon I was comfortable with. Rune mentioned goblins in his story with Nyx, so I already planned on strapping myself with sharp objects.

We talked about the nature cores and who could have the onyx essence but the truth kept its distance. It would come to us in time, but for now I was grateful to have someone on my side. My burden didn't feel so heavy now that it was shared.

"I'll keep looking. See if I find anything suspicious in our history. I'll even check these books out about Verin and his goons. I'm sure magic died because of him. It's the only logic that makes sense."

She had mentioned that; magic fell the same day mankind did. No one on either side knew why.

Great, another mystery for us to riddle out.

Chapter Twenty-Six

His breath tickled her neck as he pushed her hair away to open space for his lips to press against the tender spot underneath her ear. Goosebumps rose over her flesh as she leaned into his chest behind her.

They shouldn't be here, shouldn't be touching. But they couldn't stay away, like magnets drawn to each other, unable to resist the pull toward a mate.

"I thought you were going to break your brother's neck today." The words came out as more of a breathless moan than a statement.

The growl that vibrated against her skin made her fingers clench her dress so hard she'd probably caused a tear. It was better than touching him right now.

"You're mine," he snarled against her.

She was. He owned her heart and soul, but the politics . . .

"We can't." She tried to resist like she had for months, but her resolve was failing.

> *"It's too late." It pained him to say it as much as it hurt her heart to hear the truth in his words.*

My eyes drifted open to the sounds of a log in the fireplace breaking into embers. The dream. It was no hard guess who had played the starring roles in my head. With thoughts of Rune and Nyx rolling through my mind, I couldn't stop thinking about them. My perception of Rune had changed.

His history with Nyx reminded me of Mariam's romance stories she had kept in her room. A forbidden love, where even now they couldn't be together. After a twenty-year separation, he still looked at her like she was the love of his long life. His mate.

Knowing I'd have to be up soon to train, I massaged my leg. The cut had already healed shut and a pink scar had formed. The salve eased the miniscule pain. Rista was indeed a magical healer, even without the true magic in her hands to do the work.

I now cleaned my clothes in the laundry area instead of my bathtub, so I had a choice of a few outfits for today, including my yoga pants and shirt from when I first arrived. Not sure why, but I wanted to cling to something familiar, something not from this world.

A nonbanging knock came promptly when the sun crested over the Hallowstags, and without even answering, I knew that Celestine's words spoken two days ago had come true. Rune was not on the other side of the wooden door. Someone else was here to train me.

He was tall, like the general, but had short red hair and brown eyes. The laugh lines next to them were a signal that this Fae was not like his brooding friend.

My suspicion was confirmed mere seconds later. "Oh, this is going to be fun. You're more of a handful than the general led on, aren't you?" His hands rubbed down his face in a dramatic gesture.

I smiled as wide as I could to accentuate his thoughts. I was mischief with crazy curls to prove it.

"I'm Sapphira." I held out my hand, his own clasping mine instantly.

"Najen." And just like that, my day became uplifted after dreaming of the forbidden mates.

We left for the fighting courtyard. No waterfall fighting with Najen was on the agenda.

I was thankful for his training because he was so open. Others found me curious enough to offer their own advice and tips on fighting. By the time we finished, I knew how to get out of four different holds and where to strike the body to drop it and keep it down long enough to run away. I smiled and laughed with the guards practicing with me, feeling accepted. I wasn't only human in these Fae's eyes anymore. They watched me work hard, sweat, and bleed a little to learn. When I fell down on the dirt-coated stones, I got back up and asked for more.

In only a matter of hours, I'd earned their respect.

Najen said I was good to go eat and work with the servants after I cleaned myself up, which I was glad to do so. He didn't escort me around like he was worried I was going to cause problems with other Fae or the palace. In half a day, I'd earned his trust.

I sat at a table in the kitchen eating eggs and two slices of bacon when the head servant told me to take the day off. "We're good here. Since your injury, you haven't had an official day off." The plump Fae set a cup of water down next to my plate and winked before walking off.

Celestine's reputation as a seer held true. Rune was gone, and I had time to go exploring in the woods for some mystery creature. I finished eating and went back to the fighting courtyard to grab a bow and quiver with a sword to strap to my hip. No one acknowledged me, which sent shivers up my spine. Had Celestine somehow told everyone to let me do this?

I walked away from the palace, waiting for someone to jump out and haul me back by my hair. No one did. The suspicious feelings drifted away the closer I got to town . . . the same town I'd been watching out my window since I first arrived. The townspeople were friendly, like I imagined. Even when I told them I couldn't afford anything, artisans continued to welcome me to Crysia and discuss their inspirations from nature and Fae.

I loved immersing myself in the electric atmosphere of the town, but the sun toward the trees and my light was running out. I said goodbye to the couple I had been talking to about their pottery and made my way toward the mysterious entrance to the Hallowstags.

Chapter Twenty-Seven

As far as I could tell, the only difference between the trees of the human realm and this one was the height. Tall trees stretched up toward the clouds with large branches. Some even touched the ground as if the weight of holding their limbs was too great.

The survival instincts I'd gained from crossing the continent kept me cautious of danger from every direction. The sense of my surroundings hadn't softened by the palace life and a full belly. An eerie silence settled over the woods, as if the trees themselves stopped swaying in the wind to watch me. Each being of energy decided if the plant life and creatures of the Hallowstags could be true to their nature with me around. I'd doubted a human had ever stepped foot in these lands.

I walked to a weathered tree, its limbs hanging low. Holes marked its old age, and I placed my hand against its scratchy bark. I'd been taught in my younger years the purposes of trees. They created the oxygen we breathed and provided shelter, fruit, and materials for a community to thrive. Mariam had always told me to thank the Earth for what it provided us with nothing desired in return. She believed if mankind hadn't taken the planet for granted, things wouldn't have been so bad. I'd seen it all on the journey. Mankind had trashed the Earth. "Thank you," I whispered to the tree.

I heard rather than saw the Hallowstags reaction to me. A whirling sound from behind me coasted by, then disappeared. My body spun quickly, my hand going to the hilt of my sword in case it was not a friendly creature making the sound.

Nothing. The woods were as empty as they were moments before. At least I'd chosen to be thankful in the moment instead of fearful of the silence around me. I walked on the silent feet I'd used for many days with Tor, careful not to alert anything not relying on the sense of smell that I was nearby.

An echo of bubbling water broke the silence as I walked deeper into the woods. My shoulders sagged in relief. The taste of cool water against my dry throat was enticing, and a break sounded like a good idea. The creek was small and ran into a swimming hole, big enough to strip to your undergarments and cool off in the summer heat.

However, there wasn't any heat or wind here. I sat on a gray boulder near the swimming hole and looked into the water, making sure no creature with sharp teeth waited for me to touch the serene surface and eat me.

"I've survived the apocalypse, Dramens, Rune's personality, and an onyx tomb attack. There is no way I'm going down by a fish," I mumbled to myself to calm down, easing my growing tension. My senses were wired and alert, and my nerves ready to respond quickly if danger approached. I remembered the constant edge of surviving, of fear, and wishing to rejoin mankind. Humans were a dying breed. Fae in this realm, even without magic, were in a good place. They were safe.

I wanted more for them . . . for us. Caught up in my thoughts, I hadn't noticed the tiny bubbles breaking the surface of the water three yards from me. If I had, I wouldn't have set my weapons next to me on the boulders. I glanced around the area, then reached into the pool for some cool, crisp water. It was flowing and not stagnant so I decided confidently that I wouldn't be sick all night after drinking some.

"Holy shit." I jumped back as two yellow eyes peered at me from the ripples below the surface. The farther away I scooted on the boulder, the closer to the surface it came until its hair and face crested the waterline.

It looked at least part Fae, with shimmering green skin and pointed ears in three places instead of one. Its wide eyes did not have eyelids. Its body was still under the water but I saw arms and webbed hands with pointed nails. I didn't know what was beneath the body below the scaled chest.

I tried not to be afraid and pushed away my instincts to run, to get as far away from this creature as possible. Every muscle in my body was tight, ready to spring into action and fight. My hand stretched slowly toward my weapons, while keeping an eye on the curious being before me.

"Hello." My voice cracked, the fear in my tone evident despite my attempt to hide it.

Its head tilted to the side, like Dris did when she was intrigued.

"I'm Sapphira." Even though Celestine said not to be afraid, I had no intention of offering a hand to shake hello.

"Do you—" Before I could ask if the creature spoke, the pointed nails dug into the boulder with enough strength to dent the stone and used its strong arms to hoist itself up toward me, mouth full of sharp brown teeth aiming for my throat.

Cursing, I flung myself off the boulder, grunting as I hit the ground and tried to get up but its nails dug into my boots. I was thankful for the forethought to wear them instead of my slippers. It hissed, it's fish-like tail swishing back and forth from the waist in an attempt to steady its body on land.

"I'm not dying by some fish creature!" I roared and kicked to get free. My weapons were out of reach. It gurgled an unholy and blood-curdling scream.

This creature obviously missed my little mumble to myself earlier. After everything I'd survived thus far, I was not going down like this. I fought and managed to get my sword free without its nails biting into my skin. Something behind me landed on the ground so hard it shuddered, and the trees swayed away from the newcomer. The water creature released my leg in a hurry and crawled back into the swimming hole. The fear I'd managed to hide before could not be contained when I twisted my head to see what shook the Earth.

A black dragon stood behind me, its mouth open. Its razor-sharp white teeth gleamed in the sun's light and the blood drained from my face. A bellow roared from its massive chest, making the ground tremble, and stopped my heart right there in the Hallowstags.

Chapter Twenty-Eight

I did not blink nor move one limb as I stared down a beast that stood two stories high. Pointed, black, scaled horns sprouted from its head, four on each side, decreasing in size as they met with its powerful jaw. Webbed points started between the horns and traveled down its long neck to its tail with a horn on the tip. The wings were tucked in close to its broad body, but I wasn't fooled—it was quick and agile. I wouldn't be able to run fast enough to escape this creature.

The gray eyes looked like smoke rolled inside its irises, smoldering me with its gaze. I expected to become a pile of embers on the ground.

Do not be afraid.

If Celestine had warned me about this creature of legend, then she was crazy. What was I supposed to do? Ask it if it liked to play fetch?

The creature's breathing remained steady as it watched me and listened to the heart beating erratically in my chest.

"Friend or foe?" I managed to croak out, feeling stupid for talking to the dragon.

His head moved closer to me with uncompromising strength. I was literally as big as its skull, maybe even smaller. My body trembled with fear as its snout came so close, the exhale of heated breath caressing my face. I wanted to cry, to curl into a ball, but I stayed still as the creature breathed in my scent. Its gaze never left me as it dropped its head to the ground at my feet, closing both eyes.

It was a submissive gesture, but my heart refused to find a normal rhythm. "I'm gonna be honest with you. I am freaking the hell out."

I spoke to the dragon, and I didn't care if it understood me or not. I needed to move, to will myself to do something. Both eyes opened, then its head lifted back to where its body sat.

Run, run, run, my mind told me. I watched as the creature stood and turned as if to walk away and kept its horned tail within my reach. Its head shifted to look back at me, then at its tail as if gesturing for me to take it. Without any hesitation, I jumped up and touched the hard-horned tail with my fingers first, then my hand.

The dragon walked into the Hallowstags with me attached to it. I had no idea where we were going, but I knew I had to go along with what the creature wanted or it'd hunt me down and roast me.

The awkward silence during our walk was strange, and to deal with my fear still rolling in my belly I talked to the dragon.

"I'm Sapphira, and I'm human, so I've never met a dragon before and you seem nice. Big, but nice."

I swear I heard the dragon huff, though it didn't turn its head from wherever it was leading us.

"Thanks for saving me with that roar back there. That fish thing was definitely going to eat me. I'm gonna kill that old seer for sending me out here. If I didn't come, then I guess I wouldn't have met you, which you are cool." Unless it ate me, then that would not be cool at all.

A bright light beamed ahead as we weaved through the trees. The canopies gave us cover from the setting sun. I saw purple first, then blue, then green, and finally yellow.

None of the other creatures in the tall grassy field looked up as the dragon stomped into the open. Colorful butterflies and deer grazed alongside horses with golden horns on top their heads.

Unicorns.

Unicorns grazed in front of me. I was fucking seeing unicorns right now.

Had I died and didn't know it? Was my body currently inside a fish creature's belly in the middle of a swimming hole?

The dragon let me take everything in. The mountains in the distance accented the magical creatures that belonged here. A river, most likely the one that led into the creek, had half-naked women sitting on the shore with their fish tails swishing in the water. They looked Fae with pointed ears and multicolored hair covering their exposed breasts. Beautiful, unlike the terrifying creature who tried to eat me.

"This can't be real." I stumbled to find words to describe the fantastical scenery. I hadn't realized that I'd dropped the dragon's tail until its head was behind my back, nudging me with its snout toward the meadow of mythical creatures.

"No, I don't wanna freak them out." I pushed the dragon's head away toward the trees behind us, but I realized everyone was looking at us. Slowly I raised my hand and waved gently, hoping they saw a friend and not a foe. Every creature resumed their movements. They didn't care I was there. Maybe having a dragon at your back was some sort of pass into their world.

I wasn't comfortable moving closer to the meadow, so I observed from afar. The dragon's breathing was a balm to my nerves, a constant rhythm to remind me this was real and not a dream. Briefly I thought this would be a nice place to come back to when I needed time away from my great destiny and the pressures it came with.

"If I'm gonna see you again, I think I need to call you something other than dragon." The dragon lifted his head off the ground.

I'm pretty sure it was a "he." The vibes I got were not female. He even grunted and huffed like the Fae men I'd met. Then I remembered the name of the man who had a rare dragon's core. He died according to the book of records but he had a strong name, and I think it needed to be given to another who housed a dragon's essence inside—an actual dragon.

"How about Desmire? In this book I read recently there was a man who held a dragon's core inside him. He passed away but the name seems like a strong one."

The dragon's stare intensified. I didn't understand if he wanted me to see or feel something from that look but I got a strange sense that he wanted to say something if he could.

"Or if you have a name, that's cool, too. Can dragon's draw? Maybe we can—" I rambled on, about to suggest the dragon spell his name in the dirt. The dragon's stare had turned from intense to something like *really?*

"Well, unless you have an issue with it, I'm going to name you Desmire." There, now that was settled. I had a dragon friend with a name.

"Now, it's getting late. Would you be so kind as to show me the way back to the palace of Crysia please?" I stood, dusted off the dirt that covered my yoga pants, and looked at the empty meadow now that the sun had set.

Desmire stood and strolled with me next to him, as we followed the path to the palace. I don't know why Celestine told me to come out here and meet my new friend, but I'm glad she did.

Chapter Twenty-Nine

The next day before the sun rose, I sneaked back into the Hallowstags to see if my new friend Desmire was near. I'm sure he knew how to hunt food, but I grabbed a fish on my way out, hoping to stay on his good side. You never knew when having a dragon as a friend would come in handy.

I made it a few steps into the woods when I heard the snap of a trap. The ground flew out from under me and the world turned upside down as I hung from a tree with a rope on my ankle.

"Let me go!" I screamed, my voice bouncing off the trunks of the trees around me.

"Not quite the catch I was hoping for," a smooth voice crooned from my right.

It was dark, but I could see enough of the Fae standing in front of me. He was tall with pale skin, medium-black hair with horns, and ears sticking up, like something you'd see on a cow or goat. He had a silver ring over his lip like a piercing. Dramens were the only people I knew that had piercings.

"Whoever you are, let me go." My demand went unheeded by this horned stranger.

"You look like a tough girl; I fear for my life if you were to be set loose. You might scratch my horns." I saw past his charade. He was a thief, conman, and a swindler. This trap was set for me. He saw me coming. If it was meant for another creature, he would have chosen to do a net, not a single knotted noose to snatch one leg and hoist the body into the air. He would never be able to keep his prey still.

"I promise not to hurt you and your poor ego if you let me go." The blood in my body was rushing to my head, and the ache would eventually turn into me passing out.

The Fae picked at dirt between his fingers, then threw a knife—my knife—at where the rope hung over the limb of the tree. It sliced with precision and I fell hard. My grunt was not ladylike nor was the string of curses I released onto the thief.

"My name is Emrys, not Cad or Thief-man as you cursed with many other beautiful words." He bowed one hand behind his back like some nobleman, a smirk on his face.

"You're trouble," I added, reaching for my weapon belt. It was gone. My eyes narrowed at the thief, who pulled his hand out from behind his back with my belt and the other knife dangling.

How the hell did he swipe that from me so quickly?

"A little mischief never hurt anyone, did it? Besides when you point fingers at someone, remember you have three pointing back at you." He leaned up against the tree and tossed the belt my way. This was all for show. He was playing games for the sake of playing them. If he really wanted to mug me or hurt me, he would have done it by now.

"What is a fine lady from the palace doing out before dawn in the woods?" he mused, crossing his leather-clad legs and black boots over one another, his posture relaxed against the tree.

"Looking for my friend."

"And your friend likes raw fish?" He pointed toward the fish on the ground, dirty from falling out of my hands when I was hoisted up the tree.

"Indeed. Now I'll take my fish and be on my way." I stomped over to the fish and snatched it before he could pull some other inconvenient trick out of thin air.

"It was nice meeting you, Sapphira. If you ever find yourself in need of a skilled spider, you can find me at the market." He lifted two fingers to his forehead in a mock salute and strolled off. I wouldn't need that prick for anything. I already had a sort of jerk friend on my roster, I didn't need another.

Did he say my name? I shifted quickly to find the Fae and demand how he knew my name but didn't find him. Instead of mulling over something I couldn't do anything about, I grabbed my stuff and started walking.

After an hour of calling out for Desmire, I placed the fish on top of a boulder. At least some creature would get use out of it. Maybe my opportunity with Desmire yesterday was a once-in-a-lifetime magical afternoon with a dragon. I doubt many Fae had been saved by a dragon or watched unicorns. Shrugging off the disappointment that I might never see Desmire again, I walked back to the palace and was met by Najen when I strolled onto the fighting courtyard stones.

"Do I need to have watchdogs on you all the time?" I knew he wasn't really mad at me.

"I don't know. All that attention might go to my head." I winked and walked over to where small hatchets were lined on a shelf.

"You weren't causing mischief?" It was his job to watch me in Rune's stead, so I cooled my taunting smile and shook my head.

"No, I took some fish down the woods to feed a creature I met yesterday. That was it." I didn't mention my run-in with Emrys.

"A creature. Only you, Sapphira." Najen shook his head.

"Can you teach me to throw these?" I asked, my fingers running over the smooth wood of the hatchet. I'd seen Tor do it once on our journey, and it looked like fun. When I had tried it, it bounced off the tree and clattered to the ground very anticlimactically.

He nodded and picked up three hatchets, then told me to stand near some of the wooden targets.

I listened to his instructions and tried hard to make sure I held the handle right and put just enough force into the throw. I sent a prayer to any higher being in the world that the blade would stick into the wood but it didn't. After five tries, I had the movement locked down, and I managed to get the axe stuck at the bottom of the target a few times.

"Rune will be happy to know you're improving so fast," Najen commented, observing the blades embedded in the wood.

Rune would only care because it meant he was closer to being reunited with his mate.

Chapter Thirty

Dris and I had been reading through books for days, without much new information. I was up-to-date on Fae history, having heard about wars with past kings, Verin, and invading Fae from across the seas. Tor's family was kind and strong. He and Nyx's marriage would make a powerful alliance between the two kingdoms.

The more I read about Verin, the more I thought he was behind the apocalypse and the Fae losing their magic. I remember Tor saying something in his stories that the Fae believed he released something unto the world and that's when everything fell apart.

I wished the Fae had photographs like I'd seen in the human world. Then I would know what he looked like. Stories mentioned his black hair peeking out from his ebony armor in battles. His army was always bound in head-to-toe armor of black and red, and they'd sweep over battlefields like a smoke of fire and death.

The evil Fae hadn't been seen or heard from him since the Fae lost their magic. An eerie silence had remained in the badlands where his palace was located. Fae were edgy at first, but after a while, whispers of his death began.

My body and mind were tired from my intense training. My slim and weak muscles were now solid and strong. My figure showed womanly curves I didn't know how to handle. I was getting better and more efficient, though. Between Rune and Najen, I was becoming a fair fighter. I didn't think I could take on an army of Dramens, but I felt confident enough that I wouldn't die in the first five seconds of a battle.

Najen told me yesterday that Rune would be back today and continue my training. I wasn't excited about being yelled at to work harder or try again and again.

This morning, like every other morning recently, I rose early from my bed, sneaked out of the palace with a fish in my hand, and crept to the Hallowstags. I hadn't seen Desmire since that one time, but I wasn't losing hope.

The woods were quiet as usual. The sun wasn't yet ready to break from darkness's hold on it, and I was OK with that. The mornings were a time of peace where I could think and not have eyes on me or the weight of failure pressing against my shoulders.

"Oh no, who told you?" I whined, seeing the dark figure standing against the tree I liked to hang out on while I waited for Desmire.

"You think I wouldn't know your every move? You're still an outsider to this place."

"Oh, good to have you back, Rune, to remind me where I stand in this world." I smirked, only feeling slightly annoyed to see his handsome, scarred face.

He smirked back, his blue eyes watching me with every confident step I made. I didn't shrink under his scrutiny this time. The general was losing his edge, or it could have been his relaxed lean against the tree or the soft slack in his normally tight jaw that had me moving without hesitation.

"What are you doing out here?" He observed our surroundings curiously.

"Waiting on a dragon." I shrugged, setting my fish on the boulder I usually left it on and walked over to the tree. I grabbed the thick limb before hoisting myself up, then sat gently.

"A dragon? No dragon has been seen in over twenty years." He looked at me in disbelief, and I shrugged again.

The silence between us was strange. He wasn't making any moves to leave, and I would stay for the hour I usually did.

"This is usually my time to think," I grumbled.

"So, think."

I hit him with my best version of his one eyebrow-up stare. "You're messing up my little morning routine being here."

"Are there things you do that you don't want another person seeing?"

His retort shut me up. It could be taken so many ways and I figured it was best to keep my mouth closed than to say something that would be used against me or teased for as long as I lived.

Then again, the possible reaction I could stir in Rune outweighed the implication of embarrassment on my part. "I can't very well release some urging tensions in my core with you watching me, can I?"

Willing my cheeks not to turn red from what I was implying I did out here, I stared Rune down with my own smirk. Maybe I'd make him uncomfortable and he'd leave.

His lips turned up at the corners, and his eyes crinkled slightly at the sides. "If you needed release, you probably would have been better off somewhere less open. Anyone could find you here."

"Hasn't happened the past couple days."

"I hope you aren't telling the truth. Some of my men were out here watching you." His face wasn't as easygoing as it was before. His eyes closed and he ran his hands down his face in exhaustion.

"Maybe I am, maybe I'm not."

I heard a twig snap in the distance. My heart started beating in excitement for the arrival of my friend that would scare Rune, but then a deer walked by moments later.

"Your mouth was not something I missed while away." Rune's words caught me off guard.

"But you missed other things?" I made myself vulnerable to the inevitable pain he would inflict.

"You remind me of her. A pain in my ass and yet . . ."

Yet? What yet? What did yet mean?

I stayed quiet, eagerly waiting for him to finish.

"You aren't afraid of me; you make me feel like a man instead of a cursed soul. She was the only other one who did that."

The arrow that shot through his heart when he talked about her changed course and hit me right in the middle of my chest. We were both being cut open in front of each other, right here in the Hallowstags.

"I don't believe you're cursed."

"She used to say that, too. The only one, actually. This scar." He ran his finger down each of the three lines over his eye. "My father burned them into me when I was twelve, so everyone who laid eyes upon me would know to keep their distance. That I was cursed." He looked off into the woods. I waited for him to continue. I didn't dare breathe too loudly or move, afraid any shift would cause him to snap out of this rare exposed look into his soul.

I couldn't believe his father did that to him. Tor's father. *His* father hurt him like that.

"It's happened a few times in our family history. Most of the family have cores of wolves or gems. Dual cores are rare. I know you saw the records and saw I had two cores. I figured you would have said something by now but you haven't, and you treated me like you had before you knew."

His emotions were unreadable to me.

"Werewolves are not treated too kindly in Crysia. Or any Fae kingdom. With my magic and Nyx's help, I was able to control it and not be plagued by the moon. Since magic is gone, I have no choice in turning or not, and the full moon is near. I'll be gone until the gibbous moon."

I nodded, unsure what would happen in those days. Would he turn into some great beast and eat anyone who crossed his path?

"I'll spend my days in a cave chained to the walls until it's over. Najen will be continuing your training while I'm there." His moment of vulnerability was ending, but we'd cross some line and I wasn't going back. I'd seen another side to him . . . a better side. It was time I let him see a mirror part of himself in me.

Chapter Thirty-One

"I had been on my own for a while when Tor found me. The community I'd grown up in was destroyed by Dramens. I don't know if you know about them or not, but they are the elite in the human realm now. Awful people who either want to kill you, eat you, sell you, or breed you." I poured out things I'd never spoken aloud, not even to Tor. Tor would think he failed me if I'd told him this story, and that would devastate him.

Rune would not see me as weak. He had suffered by the hands of his family, and people feared him for being alive. I'd seen the sneers around him when people didn't think he was watching. I know he saw it, too. He saw everything.

"They raped the woman who raised me and forced me to watch. They beat me in places that could not be seen, since they wanted to sell me for some iron. They ended up changing their minds about using me as soon as they were done with Mariam."

Memories flashed through my mind like it was happening in front of me all over again. Mariam's tear-stained cheeks and her mouth crusted with blood on the corners, telling me in a hoarse voice to fight, to run. I tried, as they grabbed my clothes and ripped them off me. I tried.

"My fingers managed to grip onto a broken shard of wood from a chair nearby and I stabbed the man who had his hands below my waist while he was touching himself. It was the first time I'd killed someone. I ran, naked, until I collapsed in some bushes for the night. I'd cried and cried silently so the Dramens wouldn't find me.

"I eventually went back to the community to find Mariam. Her body had been left behind. I couldn't do anything for her, so I packed a bag, dressed, and kept moving. I was in a neighboring town raiding a house for supplies when Tor found me. He took care of me, protected me, and lifted me when I wanted to give up. He told me stories of this place but made it seem like they weren't real, like he was only human. I want to hold his lying against him, but he sacrificed himself so I could get here. Maybe Celestine told him I was going to save the princess and that's why. I'm not really sure, anymore."

I suffered from nightmares of the blond Dramen's face above me every night until I came to Crysia. Telling this story to Rune made me question everything with Tor . . . every word he said, every kiss. Was any of it real or part of the charade as a human? Tears streamed down my face without permission. I didn't want to cry and show weakness.

A warm hand touched mine on the tree's limb. Rune looked at me in awe, not with pity or sadness. "You have a warrior's core, human or not." He said those words like they were fact, instead of his opinion.

"I don't feel like a warrior." I laughed honestly, my hand gripping his like it was the only tether to my sanity.

"We can sense it, from one warrior to another. I see the fighter in you."

"Better watch your compliments, General, or I might get a big head and think I can take you down." I laughed again, trying to lighten the heavy air settling between us.

He huffed in a teasing way and pulled me off the branch with our joined hands.

"Hey!" I protested and yelped in surprise as Rune tossed me over his shoulder and carried me out of the woods.

"Your dragon isn't coming, so off to work on your skills we go." I smacked his back trying to get free from his strong arms, but his grasp on the back of my legs didn't budge. I knew why he was acting like this; he wanted to lighten my mood and take me out of that dark place I was heading. It was strange to see him so playful, but his plan worked.

"You're acting like a caveman," I groaned and pinched his backside, which in hindsight I probably shouldn't have done, but I couldn't take it back now.

"Shush, human." He popped me with his large hand on my bottom, making me shriek and wiggle to get free.

"Who are you and what did you do with grumpy Rune?" My shrieking turned to giggling at what this must look like from an outsider's view.

He didn't answer me but took off with Fae speed toward the palace with me over his shoulder, then in what seemed like one minute, he dropped me to my feet at "our" waterfall.

"Najen said you had improved. Show me what you learned." There were weapons set along the bank of the river, and while I thought about showing him how good I was getting with throwing axes, I decided it was time for a little payback. I shifted my feet for an offensive stance. Rune cracked his neck, smiling at the prospect of pummeling me into the ground.

"I'm gonna show you how it's done, old man. Two hundred years probably makes them old joints ache."

I was talking a big game, and I prayed to whatever powers that be I managed to take him down just once. Once! It was all I was begging for. He could knock me down twenty times but if I got him down one time, I would be victorious.

He didn't smack talk back with me. Instead he analyzed me and my breathing for his advantage. I hopped from side to side toward him, hoping to catch him off guard when I threw my right fist out for a punch, but he was ready. I expected it and lifted my knee into his path, connecting with a hard abdomen. His head shifted to look at me, then smiled so bright I thought my heart stopped beating for a moment.

I'd got him, and he'd smiled!

The distraction was my undoing, and Rune grabbed my arm and rolled me over his back to the solid ground. With quick feet, I jumped up and came at him again. My body angled in a spear tackle to his waist, like Najen taught me. Rune lost his footing. My body was small but the momentum of my attack had us toppling over, fighting for who would come out on top.

He did, of course, but I wasn't done. With skills of an acrobat, I lifted my hips, using my newly strong core to wrap my right leg around his neck and shifted my weight.

"Shit!"

His curse gave me all the motivation I needed to throw every ounce of my body weight into the move where I had him beneath me with my knee against his throat. I did it! I couldn't believe it.

"That's right, Grandpa!" I shouted in victory.

"You forgot an important lesson." He wasn't grinning, as his focus shifted to my heaving chest, then my face. His throat bobbing, and his breathing was as labored as mine.

"Oh yeah?" I pressed my knee into his throat a tiny bit more, showing dominance in this position.

"It's never a win until your opponent is incapacitated."

He moved his hands lightning fast, and I was beneath him in seconds, his broad body flush against mine. He didn't gloat, and I couldn't mutter a word or a breath. His face was close to mine, close enough I could feel his breaths heating my cheeks. A trembling gasp rushed from my lips at the contact of his hard body settling over mine, gravity pushing us closer than we'd been before.

His gaze moved from my eyes to my lips, and my chest seized. Wandering thoughts drifted toward his face, his perfectly hardened face. The three scars his father gave him didn't hinder his beauty. In fact, they fit him . . . the warrior with the romantic's heart. Every nerve was sensitive, and I wanted to feel those warrior's lips pressed against mine.

My gaze moved from his parted mouth to his ice-colored eyes. So many emotions and questions swirled inside their frigid depths. It was mirrored in mine . . . the desire, the pull toward him in this moment. He lit something inside me that I'd never felt so strongly before.

I *knew* . . . I knew this inexplicable draw could never be.

"You got me. Good job, Rune." I wiggled to get out from under him. He didn't fight me. He rose to his feet and held his hand out for me to take, but I couldn't chance touching his callused fingers. I was burning too hot, and I didn't know what to make of it besides the fact I wanted to toss my heated body into the cool river.

"I learned how to axe throw, too. I'm pretty good." I walked over to the axes and lifted one up, sparing one glance at Rune.

His glare was unreadable, and his body was rigid. But I knew he was feeling the same emotions streamlining through my mind.

Complete, unexplainable confusion.

Chapter Thirty-Two

I stared at Princess Nyx while cleaning her onyx tomb again. This time there would be no climbing expeditions or anything that would land me in the healer's quarters. The job was still mine, apparently. It was better I get hurt than one of the other servants since I was still low on the ranking system. I didn't mind. This was a good thing for me. I needed to see if there were any more clues as to how to rescue her.

What secrets in the onyx was she hiding? I puzzled for over an hour about her jewelry and the dark blue rock concealed beneath her perfectly manicured hands. There had to be some key story or information I hadn't stumbled upon yet. Something that when I finally figured it out, it would connect all the random dots in my head.

The ring on her marriage finger was a tiger's eye band, which meant either Rune and Nyx were married or they had intended to be.

The light blue bracelet may have been a gift from Tor. It fit the description of turquoise, his gem core, and there were two men who were fighting for her heart. Each had a gem core with the powers to create those pieces of jewelry for her.

Rune and Nyx were mates. I blushed, as if she stared at me through the crystal shield in accusation, like she knew I thought about her mate's lips on mine, his warrior's body against my own.

The whole situation was confusing. I loved Tor, but if I really delved deep inside myself, I knew something wasn't right between us. Something was missing within me that he hadn't been able to reach . . . an unyielding force or unnamed longing in my heart he had not possessed, as much as I wanted him to.

Then I thought of Rune. He wasn't mine, either. He couldn't be. His mate, the unrelenting bond between two people, lay right here, the half to another soul.

Whatever feelings stirred in my chest for the general would need to be taken out back and stabbed. Once I freed both Tor and Nyx, then we could go our separate ways . . . Rune and Nyx, me and Tor, a half-Fae male who loved me. We were good together. My stomach churned at the thought, so I focused on scrubbing the onyx harder, and avoided Nyx's face out of guilt.

The woman would likely be able destroy me if Rune's description of her fighting skills were anything to go by. Hopefully I wouldn't find out, they would be together and all would be right in the world. The end.

I was wired and on edge by the time I finished cleaning, too hyped to go to sleep and afraid of what I might dream of . . . or who. After dropping the cleaning supplies off in the closet they belonged in, I strolled quietly through the halls toward the library where Dris was organizing a shelf. I'm sure it was perfect to begin with but she liked to fuss.

"Hey you." I announced myself into the large room and she smiled.

"I was lost in thought. Good thing you showed up or I might have been here for hours." She placed a book in a selected spot and hopped down off her three-step ladder. Her landing made no sound, exactly what I'd expect from an owl Fae. Quiet and gentle.

"Did you need something? Find out more to the many mysteries we have?" Dris would be a good detective, always looking for clues or solving a mystery. A Sherlock Holmes of the Fae world.

"Nothing yet. I wasn't ready for bed. I thought maybe we could go down to the market and get something to eat together. I don't have any money but this woman who owns a little bakery said I could come eat something as long as I did the dishes. I totally do that." Even though my night would end with more cleaning, I hoped Dris would be enticed to go with me if I dangled bakery treats in the deal.

"Oh yes! That sounds wonderful. I'll get my coat. You might want to get one, too. I'll walk with you to your room, then we can go together." She vibrated with excitement, and I smiled from the happiness she stirred inside me. Pushing all thoughts of guilt and turmoil out of my mind, I decided to enjoy this outing with her.

She covered up in a light blue jacket, then we went up to my small quarters where I grabbed a hooded cape to keep the night chill away.

"I haven't had a friend to go out with in ages. Most people find me odd. Always more interested in books than parties or boys. Who has time for those, anyway? I much prefer going on epic adventures with the characters I read about." Dris slipped her arm around mine, and we walked together out of the palace and down to the market, arms linked like the best of friends.

"Well, I find you awesome, book nerd and all." I winked and pointed toward the bakery that had scents of sweet cinnamon and bread dancing in the wind, calling to us like a siren to her captain.

Laura, the baker, greeted me with a large hug that enveloped Dris as well between those big arms.

"You came back! And you brought a friend!" she exclaimed in our ears. Dris looked over at me with a nervous grin on her face. Poor librarian was probably not used to being hugged like this. Me? I soaked it in, having missed being embraced by someone who cared.

Laura was a kind soul, who donated her spare time to helping the young Fae by teaching them how to cook with free classes. When my destiny was accomplished, I was going to take one of those classes and learn how to make all the neat treats she had on display.

"All right, what would you girls like? I pulled some cinnamon buns out of the oven. Come, come, look around." Laura led us into her store to peruse, telling us about each treat with mouthwatering details. I wanted to tell her I'd take a bite of everything, but even after looking at all the treats on display, I kept going back to the cheese pastry with red cherries on top.

I didn't even have to mutter that I'd chosen the dessert before one appeared on a green plate in front of me.

"I had a feeling you were a cherry girl." Laura held the plate out for me to take, which I did like it was a gift on that holiday Mariam always tried to celebrate . . . Christmas or something jolly like that.

"Thank you." My soft voice was enough to satisfy the baker as she rushed off to get Dris a pastry called a bear claw.

We sat outside under a torch and nibbled on our treats, while people watched.

"I've never had anything like this in my life!" Dris moaned over her bear claw, and I nodded in agreement. This cherry pastry wasn't like anything I'd ever tasted.

"That's 'cause you've never tasted me, darling."

My moan turned into a groan as a familiar man pulled back the only open seat at our café table, then plopped his leather-clad backside in it.

Chapter Thirty-Three

"Emrys. What do I owe the pleasure?" I refused to let him spoil my night out with Dris. "Dris, this is Emrys." I waved between them in introduction. Emrys's hand touched Dris's and brought it to his pierced lip for a gentleman's kiss.

Her half-sneer was comical.

"Two ladies out for a late-night pastry. It's obvious you are either scheming or gossiping. I am game for both." He pulled a chocolate cookie out from underneath the little table like it appeared by magic although he had stolen it.

"I hope you're going to pay her for that somehow." He grinned while bringing the cookie to his lips slowly and savored it with an actor's flair of enjoying the morsel.

"I'll pay her however you were going to," he said, somehow knowing I was without money.

"How do you know so much about me?" I raised my eyebrow in curiosity.

"I'm a spider." He shrugged.

Dris lifted her chin slightly as she whipped out the definition from that big brain of hers. "Spider, also known as a spy. They can get into places that others cannot, they hear things that people prefer they not, they have sticky fingers, and are usually loyal to themselves. He is also a goat Fae, which is a very mischievous creature. But they are honorable, curious, and fearless."

My walking library did not disappoint.

"And she's smart, too. You are the perfect package of smart and sexy." He winked at Dris and she rolled her eyes, not impressed by this so-called spider.

"So, what does a spider want with me? There seems to a be a pattern of you barging in on my life." I took another bite of my pastry and waited.

"I may have been in the woods looking for something when I heard Celestine talking to you when you first arrived. I may or may not have heard about your destiny to save Prince Torin and release Princess Nyx from her onyx tomb."

That son of a—

"Since I obviously have many talents that can help this extraordinary task, I offer my services to you."

I scoffed at how ridiculous he sounded. "Why?" There remained so much doubt when it came to considering his offer to be truth.

He pondered over my simple question, eating another piece of the chocolate cookie. "What you're doing will be written in the history of our people. There's more to this story than a simple rescue. Something big is afoot, and I want to be a part of it."

I believed him.

"We aren't exactly going to be stealing things," Dris countered, speaking when I couldn't find the words.

Emrys peered at Dris with hooded eyes, his long black lashes giving him a boyish look, like he was innocent. "You never know. You might need ears in places you cannot be or to get into somewhere you aren't wanted, like the princess's quarters, for example. If you're looking into the mystery behind Nyx, you might wanna take a peek at her stuff, see what she was up to before being trapped in that tomb."

"We aren't breaking into her room." Dris quickly slashed his idea down, hoping I would confirm.

His idea had merit, though.

"You can't be serious, Sapphira. That room hasn't been opened since the day she was put in onyx!" Her voice escalated, but she shut her lips quickly once she remembered where we were.

"It does make sense to at least look." I chewed on my bottom lip, trying to feel remorse or some sort of guilt for possibly crossing over a line of right and wrong. However, my mind became accustomed to the idea the more I thought about it. Emrys relaxed back in his seat and nodded.

"How do we know he isn't going to double-cross us?" My friend made a fair point. He had to make a compelling argument for us to trust him, even if the idea was his to begin with.

"I'll make a blood oath, which should appease you that I will do the honorable thing and help you. I may be many things but a liar is not one of them." He lifted his thumb to his pointed canine tooth and punctured a tiny hole in his flesh. A bead of blood formed on his skin.

Dris gasped, her fingers covering her mouth at the display before us.

"I take it blood oaths are a big deal?" I asked and Dris nodded, then whispered that once made they can't be broken.

"Do I need to do anything?" I waited for directions. Emrys reached over with his other hand and grabbed my left hand, bringing my thumb to his tooth, as he did with his own. It pricked, and the smallest bit of blood bubbled on top my fingertip.

"I vow to serve you, be your spy, and to never betray you as long as I live." His gaze honed on my face, willing me to accept every word as truth and believe them deep inside my soul. I did.

He pressed our thumbs together and his vow bound us together, like some sort of magic intertwining our fates together.

My lips parted. "You don't even know me," I whispered.

"I know enough."

I now had a trusted spy on my side. "Well, this is all crazy to me. I might regret these words later when you annoy the hell out of me, but I'm honored."

He released our joined hands and smirked at Dris. She didn't blink or move.

"Dris, you OK there?

"Yep. Yep. So, when are we breaking the law and snooping through an unconscious woman's room?"

The three of us laughed. Nothing like breaking and entering to solidify lasting friendships.

Chapter Thirty-Four

"I really didn't think we were going to do this tonight," Dris whispered as we walked back up the stone trail to the palace after doing the dishes. Emrys had helped, too, and it was an odd sort of trio we made—a human, a librarian, and a spy walk into a bakery. Sounded like a joke.

Our plan was simple: Walk up to her unguarded room and Emrys would get us in. Dris said the doors were locked when the princess was entombed, so there was no real danger in this mission. However, the room was around the corner from the queen's, so the hall might be guarded. Emrys was taking a back way and meeting us inside.

"It's late. Most everyone is asleep, so it's the perfect time. . . . covered by darkness." I was sweating beneath my cape despite the chill outside. I was nervous as hell of getting caught and punished for illegal actions. Being the potential savior of the princess would only get me so far.

As always, the guards didn't pay me or Dris any attention. What mischief could a book nerd and a human servant really get into?

We walked up the servants' stone stairs. I had been stuck cleaning the bottom level of the palace, so this was quite an adventure for me, seeing more of the exquisitely designed home of the queen. The hallways were carved with swirls and patterns. Each metal torch handle was custom-made to match the walls they were nailed into. The floor had a purple rug all the way down the hall. My floor was bare basics of stone walls and stone tiles on the floor. The royal section of the palace was lavish in every way.

I heard guards mumbling from the direction of the queen's quarters, but unless we made a loud ruckus, they wouldn't be alerted to our visit.

"Perfect timing, ladies," Emrys whispered behind us. I had to reach my hand over Dris's mouth to stop her scream from echoing down the hall to the guards.

We stilled, listening for signs they had heard us, and they still mumbled.

"You jerk," Dris said to Emrys and smacked his shoulder.

These two were going to be a handful for me, although I had to admit their back and forth was entertaining.

"OK, spider goat Fae, do your stuff." I pushed Emrys toward the princess's door. Emrys rolled his eyes and began picking the lock with a criminal's finesse. It popped open almost as soon as he got started, and a smug grin appeared on Emrys's face.

"I'll make sure they put you in the books as the criminal who once opened a door." Dris pushed him out of the way, and we entered the room together. Emrys grabbed a torch from behind us since the room was very dark, and no light could enter past the thick, closed curtains.

Nyx's tomb was pretty and didn't feel final in many ways, like she was sleeping, waiting for true love's kiss from the storybooks to wake her. But looking at her room, it was like she'd been dead for centuries. The real tomb was here, in her quarters. Spider webs and dust covered every inch of this once magnificent place. Her bedspread of gold and blue had swirls sewn in across its comfortable material. A canopy of silk hung from her large wooden four-poster bed, and beside it was a pile of books resting on a table. Books were also scattered across the floor, like she'd been unable to sleep. She had a wardrobe bursting with fancy clothes covered in dust and dirt and strings from the material fraying.

"This place looks like the real tomb," Dris murmured and I nodded. It was creepy, and it felt wrong seeing her things.

"Let's look around and get out of here," I whispered, ignoring the state of this room. Even though it gave me the chills, I peered in every direction to see if any details stood out as mystery-solving worthy.

"I've been looking for these books!" Dris hissed, her fingers running over the books piled on the table.

"I think you can forgive her for not returning them," I replied.

"She was reading some heavy stuff. Core anatomy and scientific experiments by Gregory Debaru. A genius but a madman. She was researching our history, too. Trying to find something. I think she—yep —took notes in these books. Who does that?" Although the librarian in her was upset, there had to be a huge clue in those notes.

"Anything, Emrys?" He moved around items on her vanity. Brushes and makeup sat in their organized place, waiting for the princess to begin her morning routine.

"Didn't the princess have purple hair?" he asked.

Both Dris and I nodded. I'd stared at her sleeping body enough to know that she indeed had lavender-hued hair.

"What did you find?" Silently I walked over and looked at the brush he held. It was not purple but a darker colored hair. *Odd.* I thought of excuses or an answer to this new piece of the puzzle, but I couldn't come up with anything. The princess's room was as mysterious as the woman in the tomb.

"Guys, I think I found something." Dris waved us over to the collection of pretty dresses.

"There's something under there. Look, see those markings," she continued, pointing toward the floor of the expansive wardrobe.

"I see it." Emrys reached over and pushed the petrified dresses out of the way.

"Oh, my heart tree." Dris gasped, her owl eyes widening at the madness before us, written all over the wall of the wardrobe.

"No one said the princess was mad, too." Emrys's low voice of confusion mirrored the thoughts in my head.

Scribbled on the wardrobe were words of a madwoman. Over and over. Every warning bell in my mind told me to run. Run far and run fast.

He knows.

He's coming for me.

Must split it. Must hide it.

He knows.

He's coming.

Sleep. Sleep. Sleep.

The darkness is coming.

The darkness is coming.

Chapter Thirty-Five

I stared at the books piled on the floor next to my bed, the ones Emrys and Dris helped carry down to my chamber after fleeing the princess's quarters. All three of us were silent in a mixture of confusion and fear. We were missing something but where to begin?

Nothing in the stories I'd heard mentioned the princess was mad like her mother. Her mother only went crazy after using up her powers to help put her daughter in the onyx tomb, right?

My mind hurt from all these new revelations. Dris told me she would come into my room this morning to help me search through the princess's notes. As confused as I was, another emotion rattled me more. Nyx was frightened and unhinged in the days before being locked in her tomb. Nothing on the sleeping princess's face showed fear or the madness of a woman who wrote such scary words on the back of the wardrobe. She looked at peace in the onyx. Maybe she split and hid what she wanted to or knew she was safe from the darkness in there.

The only thing I could associate the darkness with was whatever Verin released into the world. I remembered the story of when mankind fell. There was a flash of black across the sky and people died where they stood. It couldn't be a coincidence. There was a common denominator here—Verin, the evil king.

I yawned widely and loudly as I answered the quiet knock on my door. Dris wore comfortable clothes instead of the cute dresses she usually wore.

"Did you get any sleep?" I asked, seeing the dark circles under her eyes. I had tossed and turned, thinking about an unhinged Nyx until the early sun rose.

"Nope. Who could sleep after being in that room? It's scarier than the dungeons." I'd have to take her word for it since I had no interest in going down to where the dungeons were.

"It's small, but come on in. I was about to start reading." She sat on the edge of my bed, while I closed the door.

"I don't even know where to start." She looked at the pile of six books, all different in sizes and leather covers binding them. I agreed with a grimace at the difficult task before us. This wasn't going to be fun, but there had to be a reason Nyx was looking at these books before she laid down to accept her fate.

"You do those three, and I do the others?"

I separated them and set three randomly in front of her, then curled on my bed with the others. The task before us seemed vast and intimidating. I hadn't even opened a book and I grew overwhelmed.

"One page at a time, right?' I mustered up a pep talk for the two of us. Dris grinned and opened a book she hadn't touched in twenty years. To her, this was a great adventure.

The woman I'd heard about from Rune and Tor made the princess appear levelheaded, strong, and a badass. My fingers trembled slightly as I lifted the cover to the first page of the core anatomy book.

Dris and I silently read through Nyx's notes and flipped the pages with interest. I took in the information she wrote, as well as what was on the page itself. I now understood more about how the cores worked.

The Fae had the power of their nature's core, and the Fae had the ability with absolute mental control of their essence to solidify it. According to the book, since the queen's core was a diamond, she could take all of her essence and turn it into one diamond stone, probably a large one . . . like taking tiny particles and combining them to make them into a bigger substance.

"Look at this." Dris pointed to handwriting next to a painting of a dissected person.

"What the hell is that?" It was grotesque and I wasn't sure I wanted to know what the princess thought of it.

"This is the book by Gregory Debaru. It's his experiment on Fae to test how much of their essence could be taken away before they died. It's odd, but the princess found it interesting. She wrote here, in beautiful handwriting might I add, that she wondered which tools he used, or if it was his gifts that he used on the experiment, since it wasn't in his description."

Gross! Why they hell did she think she needed to know this information? We continued to read and think about the meaning of her notes. It wasn't adding up. As always, something vital was missing from the puzzle.

A knock on my door had both of us lift our heads. It wasn't loud like Rune's booming against my chambers, so it must be someone else. I gently placed the book I was reading on the bed and walked to the door. Dris resumed reading.

"Human Sapphira." A guard wearing armor stood in the hall, his face completely void of any emotion while he waited for me to fully open the door.

"Just Sapphira. Is everything OK?" It was odd having a guard here, then all the blood drained from my face. They must know we broke into the princess's chambers last night.

I took a small step back, ready to close the door if he tried to grab me, but he didn't say anything else as his hand lifted with a folded and sealed letter in his grasp. I wasn't in trouble. Relieved, I wanted to collapse against the stone tiles. My hand reached out to take the letter and as soon as I held the elegant parchment, the guard left.

"What's that?" Dris's attention was solely on my hand as I turned to shut the door behind me.

"A letter of sorts."

"That's the queen's seal." She pointed with awe.

Slight remorse tore at me as I ripped it open. The seal of Crysia was beautiful in the nearly white wax.

"She wants me to join her for tea again." I bit my lip to prevent myself from screaming excitedly.

"Oh, that's so wonderful! When?" Dris was already up and putting the books back into a pile on the ground where they were before.

"Uh, in like twenty minutes." Crap. OK. I could be ready and out to the waterfall where she requested to meet. I knew my appearance needed work, so I would do the best I could.

"I'll leave you to it then. Have fun and we will work on this later."

"You are the best. I'm really glad I have you as a friend." It was the first time either of us had said anything out loud with the title of friends, but we knew it was true.

"I'm glad you're my friend as well, Sapphira. We oddballs got to stick together." She reached over and hugged me. My arms wrapped around her petite form and squeezed. It was so nice having a friend.

"OK. Now get your human butt ready for a tea date with the queen."

Chapter Thirty-Six

Dressed in a nice pair of leggings and a thigh-length tunic with a belt around my waist, I walked out of the palace to the waterfall.

I'd tried to make my hair prettier than the curly mess it was when I woke up, except the frizziness was not working with me. It usually got extra crazy when rain was near, something I'd yet to experience in the Fae realm. I thought about the possibility of rain looking magical on the steppingstones to the waterfall, when I noticed the queen wasn't sitting on the blanket with her beautiful tea set like she was last time.

I didn't see any guards, though I knew they were around somewhere.

"Where . . ." I muttered to myself. The queen stood in the middle of the river, her hand reaching into the waterfall, which battered her delicate fingers. A diamond was the strongest of the gems, so maybe it really didn't feel like anything against her Fae hand.

The beautiful red and creamy long dress she wore was soaked up to her knees. It twisted and struggled against the surge of water trying to rip it off of her. Her attention settled on the falls, like she saw a serene image in the reflection of the water. Her expression was beautiful, like the look of a woman in love seeing her lover. A gentle smile graced her lips, not too bright, but subtle enough to know she thought of something happy.

I liked seeing her like this, even in the odd situation of the moment. The queen stood in the river, her hand in the waterfall like it whispered sweet nothings in her ear peacefully.

"What the—"

Oh, that son of a bitch.

A black snout pressed through the water into her hand. I knew exactly what was on the other side of the waterfall. Or better yet, *who* was there. Desmire played with the queen incognito. To anyone else it looked the like queen merely caressed the waterfall, the snout was barely recognizable as the dragon's. I only knew what it was because I'd seen him before.

What was he doing here? What was he doing with the queen? Why was she touching him like she knew him and missed him?

I became increasingly uncomfortable as I watched intimate relations between them. Her mouth moved, but I couldn't hear anything over the roar of the waterfall. I glanced around, unsure of what else to do, but just standing there wasn't good, either. I looked guilty, like I was watching them, and I shouldn't be. She could get mad that I'd arrived a moment before and stayed silent instead of announcing my presence.

The war waging in my mind tilted on the side of saying something, even though it would interrupt their moment.

"Queen Olyndria?" My voice was louder than I intended it to be but the tone did the job. The black snout disappeared into what had to be a cave behind the waterfall, and the queen still stood there looking at the reflection in front of her.

With haste, I walked over to Her Majesty, ready to help her in case she got swept under by the rolling waters under the falls. She gave me a sweet smile as she walked toward the blanket. The wet train of her dress collected dirt as she stepped onto the bank of the river.

"Black love sees a rat inside the palace." She sat down gingerly on the blanket, speaking with grace, the soaked part of her dress spreading into the drier spots. I handed her a napkin.

"Here's this to dry yourself, if you need it."

She didn't take the napkin and this time poured the tea for us. Her hands tremored and the tea spilled more on the blanket than into the cup, but I smiled and thanked her.

"I'm so glad you invited me; I can't explain it but I feel happy to be around you." My admission brought a pink blush to my cheeks. She continued to sip from her half-filled teacup.

"I've been training a lot with Rune and Najen. I'm getting pretty good, too. I think the hatchet is my favorite." The queen drank her tea while I talked as I did last time, telling her about my stay in Crysia, leaving out all the things I thought would upset her, like her daughter or meeting Desmire.

After our third round of tea and a tasty cheese sandwich with meat inside, a green-headed guard approached in haste toward the queen. "Your Majesty, the king has arrived from his hunt. He's eager to see you and is on his way." The guard retreated shortly after delivering his announcement.

I hadn't been interested in meeting the king after everything I'd heard about the lazy, entitled man. It was bound to happen one day, so I was glad to be near the queen now that the moment had come. Her delicate hands gripped onto my arms and pulled me toward the river. She dragged me, even though her face was still serene.

"Your majesty, please! You're hurting me!" I tried to peel her grip off me, except she held on too tight. Panic settled in my gut. The mad queen was going to hurt me. She might not even realize she was doing it. The look on her face held no malice or kindness, but she continued to drag me with her diamond strength and ignored my pleas to stop.

"Please—" She walked into the river with me, water filling my nose and mouth as I struggled to stand above the current. I gurgled a scream as the queen pushed me farther into the river toward the falls. She was going to kill me. I wasn't Fae and couldn't handle the pressure of the falls on my body.

I didn't want to hurt the queen but I couldn't let her drown me. I fought back, pushing my hips up to get me closer to the surface and out of the water. My lungs burned. I managed to come up for a second only to be pushed down by a hand on my head and dragged farther into the river.

My fingernails dug into the queen's forearms. My feet kicked and I tried twisting my body. She was strong. So strong. The beating drops of the falls in the water were close. I sobbed but did not see flashes of light to the afterlife or my sad life reeling in front of me. It was a simple acceptance that I was weaker, and there wasn't anything I could do.

Her fingers that had dug into my skin so harshly vanished and I clawed my way through the water. I pressed my hands against the stone riverbed, pushing myself up. The first gulp of air hurt. There was too much water in my chest. I swam and fought the current of the river to the bank, coughing and, struggling to find my bearings, as I barely made it the river's edge.

"I'm so sorry. Are you all right?" A warm hand brushed against my face, pushing my hair away as I tried to catch my breath, coughing up water with every exhale.

"What's your name, little gem?" The male voice crooned in my ear, like I was a child in need of coddling. I had an invasion of emotions I didn't know how to handle.

"Sapphira," I managed to bark out toward the stranger.

"Such a pretty name, little gem." The man helped me to my feet like I weighed nothing, his hands moving to my face.

He was a tall Fae with pointed ears, long black hair, and golden eyes, bright and beaming. He had sharp features and medium brown skin, a shade darker than mine, and wore a golden crown with a black obsidian stone resting in its middle on top his regal head.

"King Lachan."

The king had saved me from death's embrace.

Chapter Thirty-Seven

"I can't believe the queen tried to drown you and the king saved you. I mean talk about a wild tea party." Dris played with my hair, trying to make it look halfway decent for tonight.

Once the king had hoisted me to my feet, he looked at the queen in a way a father would look at his troubled daughter. His pursed lips indicated disappointment, but she wouldn't face any repercussions from her actions. I was a human, and she was the queen.

The whole thing made me feel so much, and yet I tried to close the memory off like it hadn't happened two days ago. The king had patted me on the back like I was a small child and invited me to the welcome home ball that night in his honor. She stood behind him, soaking wet, her face impassive. I wanted to shout at her, to shake her, and ask her why. But I couldn't and my mind had trouble accepting the fact there was nothing I could do to reach her.

I didn't have anything to wear to a Fae ball, although Dris said she would find me something and help me do my hair after I was done with my servant's duty.

A green dress rested on my bed waiting for me. It looked nice, and it fit well when I'd tried it on when Dris first came to my room. It wasn't as extravagant as some of the dresses I'd seen before at the other ball, but it was nicer than anything I'd worn in my life.

"Well, no matter what the queen did, I'm glad you are here, and I'm super excited you'll be at the ball tonight. Maybe I'll go with you so you can have a buddy, though I normally don't go to those types of parties." She pulled on the tender hair at the nape of my neck, making me hiss though I didn't tell her to stop. I trusted she would make me look beautiful, so I could bite back every sensitive pull of hair as she designed.

"I'd like to have a friend there, but I understand if you don't want to." I spoke through clenched teeth. Messing with curly hair was not relaxing, and it felt like she was trying to rip it out.

"I will. It won't take me long to get ready. I've had to do it a time or two."

Someone knocked on the door, and Dris jumped up to answer it before I could speak. "I'll get it." Dris patted my head, and I stayed as she opened the door and peered from side to side. No one was there, but a box sat on the ground.

"You've got a present!" she exclaimed, her pointed fingers grasping the edges to lift it with ease.

"Is there a note or anything?" My chin lifted, hoping I'd see more of the box and a piece of paper stuck to it somewhere, though after a minute of looking I didn't see anything.

"Maybe it's from your general." Dris winked and I scoffed, partially regretting that I'd told her about our little moment. Since I had been emotional about the queen trying to kill me, I'd let the other frustrations in my life slip out.

Rune hadn't been the one to train me lately, although I'd seen him talking to guards and the king.

Ever since the king arrived, people were caught in a whirlwind of chaos, working harder, cleaning with more precise movements, and making the palace more alive than it was with the queen. Everyone knew the queen was mad and thought they could slack off and she wouldn't notice. With the king back, everyone was thrown into a tizzy. He could see if they weren't working and decide their fates.

In the moments I'd been in his proximity, he seemed relaxed and easygoing. His golden eyes lingered on my face and clingy wet clothes for a moment longer than necessary. Although I'd read in human history about kings who had many wives and never stayed true to their queen, the thought was gross. Hopefully, if all went according to plan, I was going to avoid King Lachan's lingering gaze as much as possible.

"Open it!" Dris's excited demand brought me back to the current situation. The mystery box. My eager fingers touched the seam of the lid and pushed up. A collective gasp echoed around my tiny room.

"I don't care who sent it, you are definitely wearing it." Dris's hand reached out like she wanted to touch the soft, white fabric but stopped, then as if being pulled, her fingers moved over the dress lightly as a feather. The dress had a black line tracing the sweetheart neckline, then fading into off the shoulder straps.

Dris helped me gently lift the dress out of the box and hold it up for a better look. I couldn't fight back my smile. It would hug my every curve, then flare out slightly at the knees. A black sparkling tree design spread on the right side all the way up to the breast segment. Against where my ribs would be were two gems that had a sheer black train that would follow in the wake of my every movement.

It was a dress of dreams . . . my dreams.

"Is this real?"

"It looks like the forest after a winter's storm. You need to put this beauty on, like right now."

She didn't have to tell me twice. I stripped while she helped me slide into the snug dress and fastened it.

I normally was not vain, but for once, I wished I had a mirror so I could see myself in this strange woman I'm sure I resembled. Obviously, the person who would be staring back at me with those forest eyes was not the Sapphira I knew. Maybe for the night I could smile, laugh, and dance and not be a woman who had to save a princess and prince.

"We need to finish this hair and then get to that ball; it's probably already started. But you have to wait for me because I wanna see all those haughty Faes' faces when you walk in." I heard her words but I relished in the luxury over this dress against my skin, allowing me to feel confident and powerful.

Dris put the majority of my curls into a low bun at the top of my nape. Little tendrils of curls roamed free as she pulled out little silver clips the size of twigs or coral from a bag she had brought with her. She placed them strategically in my hair. Once she was satisfied with her handiwork, she left to put on her own dress and told me she'd meet me down there.

I sat on the bed, looking up at the sunset. It was going to be a full moon tonight, and despite knowing that I shouldn't, I lifted up the train of my dress and left my room for another.

Chapter Thirty-Eight

Rune's quarters were on the opposite side of the palace near the woods. I'd seen it a few times, and the servants I worked with usually ushered me to do the cleaning near his room. I think they were afraid of him and thought that he'd open his door and chew them up.

My stomach twirled into a ball of knots as I stepped closer and closer to his wooden door. The torches outside were dimmed, which made me regret my decision. I couldn't shake the desire to see him, especially while wearing this dress that gave me courage and strength.

I knocked and heard the scrape of a chair against the stone floor, then Rune flung the door open. His bare torso revealed the muscles of his ripped abdomen, with only a pair of pants covering the rest of him. He wore a necklace on a simple silver chain with a black circle pendant. I'd never seen him wear jewelry, so the necklace was odd.

"What do you want?" he snapped, the furrow between his eyebrows growing deeper. He did not like what he saw. *Shocking.*

"Tonight is a full moon, and I hadn't seen you the past few days. I wanted to say goodbye before you left for your werewolf cave thing." My heart throbbed with the thought of him suffering alone.

He didn't say anything as I noticed his broad chest, abdomen, and so many muscles and ripples of pure strength and brutal training weaved into his body. He radiated the beast inside. A true warrior, who'd fought in battles and had the scars on his body to prove it, including the one small white dot on his shoulder from Nyx's sword when they first met.

I shouldn't have come here tonight. I was wrong for looking at him like this, for wanting to wish him goodbye. The pull, the something inside me refused to listen.

"Well goodbye." I turned to leave and flee the scene of my betrayal.

"I couldn't be near you. I'm sorry I stayed away." His strong hand grabbed my wrist and stopped me from leaving. My head snapped to look at him, at his stretched arm and grip attached to me.

"I thought we were friends." I tried to bring the conversation back to neutral territory.

"We are," he groaned, his hand releasing me like the mere touch of my skin had scalded him. His fingers moved through his hair as he peered up at the skies like some assistance would come to him from above. Little spikes of black hair poked up from his fingers gripping the strands. My body shivered from the craving to replace his hands with my own, to feel his silky ebony hair between my fingers, gripping him closer.

Heat blossomed in my chest; my breaths trembled with another full body shiver. His nostrils flared, his hands moved from his hair to the doorway. The powerful, corded muscles in his arms flexed, like he needed all his strength to root his feet where they belonged.

Why did my body and soul yearn to do something I wasn't sure I could come back from? It felt right, though, and I couldn't explain it. I'd experienced that overwhelming desire back at the waterfall when his body settled over mine, his air becoming my air, my cravings echoing inside his icy stare.

"I wish I could be with you in there, Rune, so that you'd know you weren't alone."

A small sigh escaped his lips. The sound crushed something in my chest. The need to reach out to him, to soothe him, tore at my control. Every breath turned into a fight to hold back the words that would doom me.

"Goodnight, Sapphira." His strangled voice was filled with suffering.

I shouldn't have come. The dress was not some mask that hid my flaws and vulnerabilities like some superhero. I was open for Rune to see, and it felt wrong.

"Goodnight, Rune," I whispered.

His door shut, as I walked back through the hall. My thoughts and emotions scattered with the draft flowing out to the throne room, where the laughter and murmuring of the celebrating Fae congregated.

Dris stood by the entrance in a shimmering silver dress that looked like stars. Her wild hair was free, and she wore matching silver shoes to complete the ensemble. I plastered on my best smile, hoping to deter her from asking questions of why I looked like I'd been attacked. She saw through it. The owl essence in her was too keen at seeing things beyond what was obvious, but her pink lips remained sealed.

Her arm linked around mine in a friendly way that I understood with gratitude. She was here for me, my friend, and to be there for anything I needed, like entering a throne room of Fae who looked at me with a mixture of hunger and disgust in their eyes.

"I don't think this was a good idea," I whispered, hoping the others weren't listening to me as we walked up the dais where the king and queen sat on their respective thrones. The king dressed his lithe body in an all-white tunic and black pants. His long black hair was unbound, and his crown of obsidian sat happily on his head.

The queen peered down at her hand, her lips moving like she mumbled, and tears stung my eyes. I wanted to hate her for what she tried to do, but I couldn't harbor any emotion toward her except to love and please her.

"Sapphira, welcome. I'm glad you could make it, and I'm so happy the dress fit you so stunningly."

The king had officially ruined this beautiful garment that covered me like his personal present, wrapped how he wanted me to be. The food I'd ingested earlier threatened to come back up the way it went in.

The sour churning in my stomach made me want to run to the nearest bathroom I'd cleaned many times and rip off this dress as I vomited.

"She is most grateful, your highness. You are very kind." Dris spoke for me and pulled my arm so the rest of me would fall into a bow with her. The king's head bowed in response, as close as we were going to get to some sort of respect from him.

"Enjoy the night, Sapphira." Chills ran down my arms as the king spoke directly to me again, ignoring Dris at my side. I was thankful for her Fae senses as she noticed the king's behaviors and said our thanks before steering us toward the refreshment table.

"We are going to need something strong to get through this night." Dris poured herself some of the pink wine and handed me a glass. I hadn't drunk any sort of alcohol in a long time, so I would be a mess if I drank a lot. One drink wouldn't hurt me. I was in desperate need of something to numb myself.

Chapter Thirty-Nine

Turns out Fae wine was not like the alcohol humans drank. It was strong, mixed with a certain purple-colored berry that went straight to your bloodstream and turned off the inhibitions button in your mind.

Dris watched over me, and I was grateful. I laughed and danced by myself, mostly because Emrys sneaked into the ball and became a bodyguard. Anytime a curious Fae danced toward me with interest, my loyal spider blocked him with his dark eyes and sneer. I didn't mind the absence of a dancing partner. I didn't want to think about men or destinies or anything heavy.

My body was coated in a light sheen of sweat, and the music was as lovely as I'd heard the other times I was near the festivities. This time I wasn't supposed to not be seen or heard. I could laugh and smile and move to my heart's content.

I'd only had two drinks and a small finger sandwich to combat the effects of the alcohol. My only desire came in the form of lifting my hands in the air and swaying my hips along with the musicians who played a lively song.

Other Fae danced, too, and when I needed someone else to do a couples with me, I grabbed either a shy Dris or a willing showboat Emrys.

I didn't know what time of night it was, and the party hadn't slowed when I finally told Dris, "I'm going to the bathroom!" I didn't need her to go with me down the hall, so she ate an apple while Emrys danced. She tried hard to ignore his strutting like a peacock. I giggled, then stopped when I saw two bodies against the wall in a dark alcove beyond the bathroom doors.

Just as I reached the door of the restroom, I heard it . . . a loud slap of a hand against a face and heels clicking toward my direction. The queen passed by without glancing in my direction. If she was the queen, then . . . *Crap.*

"Sapphira," the king whispered in a purring tone, his body resting on the stone wall.

"Hello, Your Highness, and excuse me." I did my best curtsy or bow. I wasn't sure which I actually ended up accomplishing because my foot slipped slightly. I reached to open the door to the bathroom to get away from him, but his hand stretched so fast and pushed the door shut with all fingers splayed across the wood.

"Why did you have to come here, little gem? Something about you . . . Can't put my finger on it. The draw. Not in my plans at all." It almost sounded like a whine, as his other hand touched a tendril of my curly hair.

Instantly I took a step back, and he took another forward, crowding my space with the wall at my back.

"You look ravishing for a human. Maybe you will tell me your secrets in and out of that dress." He leaned in and I counted to ten, hoping I didn't need to assault the king because my stay here in Crysia would probably end up with me dead.

His nose touched the side of my face, the tip of it running along my cheek bone as he inhaled my scent before returning back to where he was standing. "Sapphira," he breathed, holding the "a" from my name longer for emphases.

All of the drinks and food in my stomach churned, my vision turning into a shade of yellow.

"I'm going to puke." I pushed him out of the way with too much force and ran into the bathroom to expel everything in my stomach. I was too sick to know if the king had followed me into the closed space. In a temporary break of heaving, I managed to look around and saw no one before going for another round of hurling into the toilet I'd most likely be cleaning tomorrow.

My cheek rested against the cool seat, and I let out a groan that echoed off the stone walls. I was done with the night. The king had officially ruined any sort of fun I had been having. What did he even mean by everything he said?

"I'm not ready for this shit," I muttered to myself as I climbed up to my feet and shuffled to the sink basin where I could wash my face and mouth. "What are you doing, Sapphira?" I asked myself when I got a look at the woman in the mirror. She looked beautiful, even wearing a dress that a creepy king got specifically for her. This woman looked so different from the one who had trekked across the continent.

I couldn't forget the Saphhira who should have died in my community. She was still a part of me no matter how far I traveled, how much I trained, or how dressed up I appeared. Two Fae women walked into the bathroom, laughing and tripping over each other. They pushed me out of the way to the sinks.

Dris waited where I'd left her with Emrys nearby, who had a drink in his hand instead of prancing around. She took one look at me and knew I was finished with the night.

"Are you OK, Sapphira? You look more than the type of ill you get from the wine." She pressed her hand to my head, checking for fever as I nodded her off.

"I'm fine. I'm ready to call it a night. You don't have to leave, though, if you want to stay." I hugged her, loving my friend for her caring gestures. Emrys watched us, then heard someone call his name. Quickly, he set his drink down and walked over to us, his gaze constantly shifting around the room from the people to the windows and even to the ceiling above us.

"What's bothering you, itsy bitsy spider?" I cooed, still under the influence of the wine.

"Something's not right."

The tone of his voice was full of worry. Emrys rarely looked serious. My body tensed and Dris's trembling hand reaching down to interlace with mine.

Her head darted from side to side like a nervous owl. The music stopped when everyone except me sensed a disturbance in the room.

Then it happened.

Glass shattered to the ground in an ear-piecing crash. Fae from all over the room screamed as soldiers armored in red and black descended upon the room. We froze as the men sliced all Fae in their path.

Verin's soldiers.

Chapter Forty

My fear vanished in seconds, and even intoxicated, I managed to grab one of the knives by the banquet table. It was a simple knife but could slice into evil Fae flesh, if needed.

"We need to get out of here," I told my friends, and we moved as one toward the exit where everyone else was currently rushing for their lives, trampling others in their frightened state.

Neither the queen or king were within sight, most likely having been pushed away to safety by their bodyguards. If the queen was not in her current state of mind, she would have fought off the intruders with her guards.

"Shit!" I cried out, as someone wrapped their hands around my waist and tried pulling me away from my group. The knife within my tight fingers was knocked out with unfortunate ease. Emrys came at the evil Fae with a swift kick, and I was free again.

But only for a moment.

"Get her out!" A man's voice bellowed in the room and another soldier grabbed me. This time Emrys and Dris could do nothing as two men with swords blocked their path. Dris called out my name, her hand reaching out, but then men walked close to them. Emrys pushed Dris behind his back, protecting her. He muttered something, and my friends ran as quick as their Fae speed could whisk them away. I got it and didn't want them hurt, but they left so quickly that I felt a tiny stab in my chest.

I writhed, scratched, and stepped on boots as I was dragged toward a broken window. I needed one second to get free. Then I could use one of the moves that Najen and Rune had taught me to beat a Fae and to run afterward.

I stopped fighting and breathed in, taking in the sounds, sights, and scents around me. Verin's men receded, and the queen's guards fought them back, but many had fallen on both sides. The coppery tang of blood marinated the air, and the sounds of grunts and swords clashing echoed through the room. Diamonds from the tree behind the throne clattered against the stone floors.

The man dragged me while I pretended to relax. I needed to wait until he thought I wouldn't fight back, then strike. We were almost to the window when my moment came. I struck him in the gut and stepped on his toe before using my elbow to uppercut him in the face. He released his hold to touch his bleeding nose, then with a feral glare he reached for me again. I avoided his fingers but something hit my head. Pain flared, and sounds went silent.

***

I wasn't out for long. The knock to the head made my vision blurry, and my body jostled around as someone carried me outside the palace, past the garden, toward the Hallowstags. If they got me into the woods, it would be over. I screamed as loud as I possibly could, fighting, biting, hitting, and clawing my way out of my kidnapper's tight grasp. He wasn't going to let me go.

"Shut up, bitch!" Obviously they'd been after me. I had to be getting close to fixing Verin's curse. By releasing the princess from her tomb, she would be able to save the Fae from his grasp.

Sounds of the falls came into earshot. We were going to cross the river. I screamed as the first cold rush of the river hit my skin. The soldier slowed in the strong current. One step in front of the other, he moved with an unrelenting purpose to get me far away from the palace.

Suddenly, a wall of fire grew in front of us. The soldiers scrambled back from the searing heat and flames. Another blast came and turned three of Verin's men to ash before my eyes. The scent and sight made me want to vomit again. I'd never forget the scent of a burning body nor the sight of the black ash floating down the river that was once a body.

The roar that shook the Earth came from the Hallowstags.

Desmire.

With renewed strength, I fought with more boldness than before. My kidnapper tried to move beyond the wall of fire, but Desmire blocked his advance, his teeth dripping with saliva and his gray eyes narrowing at the man holding me.

The solder didn't put me down. Instead, he tightened his grip. His wading body shifted and he ran in the water toward the opposite shore of the dragon. Crysia's guards, along with the king and queen, ran toward us.

The queen stretched her hand out to me, willing magic to come forth, but none came. The king's mouth opened and closed at the sight of Desmire.

"You!" he finally screamed at Desmire with a feral hatred. The guards hunted the scattering enemy, abandoning their plan to kidnap me.

Desmire roared, shooting fire from his mouth toward the soldier beneath my body, careful not to burn me. Knowing he was not going to win this fight, he dropped me down into the cold river, his arm going around my waist, pinning me to his hard-armored chest. Something sharp pressed against my neck, and I became still as stone. The tiniest whimper escaped my mouth.

"Let us go or I'll kill her. Verin prefers her alive but said it didn't matter if she perished," the soldier said, looking at the royals and the snarling dragon.

Desmire leashed his rage for my safety at the sight of the blade against my throat. The king still had his hate-filled gaze on the dragon and the queen muttered to herself, watching me. No one moved or talked.

"Let her go!" Dris and Emrys jumped into the water behind us, having joined the scene stealthily. However, they both stopped their movements when they saw the knife at my throat.

A small gasp bubbled from me at the prick of pain from the soldier pressing his weapon into my flesh, proving he would harm me. Warm liquid ran down my throat. I was afraid to breathe or move. This man was really going to kill me.

My eyes met the queen's. For some reason it was her eyes I wanted to see while dying . . . to know one part of her—even if she had tried to kill me—cared. I could see it in her face now, and I wished I knew what she was thinking.

The knife at my throat was suddenly gone. The soldier's fingers gripped my dress as he was dragged away from me. His grasp spun me around as he was lifted off his feet. Standing in the river, with the soldier in his clawed grip, stood Rune.

In werewolf form.

Chapter Forty-One

My legs gave out. Not even the water's chill could shake me from my stupor. I stared at the large beast standing a few feet away.

Rune roared at the soldier. His sharp white canines glistened in the moonlight, and his bulging muscles held the larger soldier with ease. His three scars were visible on his wolf-like face as he snarled. He was every bit the beast right now while the man hid inside somewhere.

With no warning and no thought of forgiveness or surrender for the soldier, Rune's snout opened wide and snapped the soldier's head off with his razor-sharp teeth. The armored body sank into the river, weighed down as a stone. The head floated down the river like a fallen leaf instead of the fear-stricken expression on a skull.

Blood coated the general's pointed teeth as he snarled. He stood on two feet, black hair covering his bulging muscles, and pointed ears shifting in different directions, listening to the crowd around us. I sat in the water unafraid. I had no reason for that gut feeling, but I knew he wouldn't hurt me.

Desmire growled, and I remembered everyone came for my safety.

"It's OK, everyone. I'm OK," I whispered, knowing everyone around me heard my words as I rose slowly.

Rune bared his teeth in a menacing way as he watched me. He took one step toward me, then another. I heard the collective gasp from my friends as Rune turned toward them and snarled again ferociously. Any normal person would collapse to the ground in fear, but not me.

I didn't back down but challenged him. I refused to move. His crinkled snout smoothed. Rune was in there somewhere. I believed it.

"Sapphira, move slowly toward us now," the king said, stretching his hand in my direction. Whatever he had done earlier was gone. He was now a concerned king for the human who was going to save his daughter.

Rune didn't trust him, either. I shook my head while looking at Rune. With confident steps in the river, I closed the distance between me and the beast. His muscles flexed, like he was fighting the urge to rip me in two like the soldier he'd broken earlier. A metal clinking sound broke the silence and I saw the broken shackles and chains on Rune's wrists.

"Sapphira!" someone shouted just as Rune grabbed me with his furry, human-like hands with sharp claws . . . not paws. I shook hard as he cradled me in one furry arm and took off in a powerful sprint away from the river. My fingers and legs gripped his long, muscled torso as best as I could, but I was being carried like a ragdoll. All my joints shook like they were going to snap with every movement Rune made toward wherever he was taking me. I knew he wouldn't hurt me intentionally, but he was not being gentle in his current state.

A tree branch smacked into my head and I passed out in Rune's jostling hold.

***

Warm . . . safe . . . protected . . . until the pain of my injuries woke me from my temporary coma.

I had to have a concussion or some sort of fracture in my skull from the two times I'd been knocked out. I peeked through closed eyes and didn't see any torches, only the moonlight shining brightly on the rugged stone floor of a cave. As I tried to get up, a large furry arm tightened around my torso.

The breath in my lungs stilled as I saw a massive werewolf arm holding me tight, the other one curled across my chest, like he was holding onto his favorite possession. My head lifted to see if he was awake. However, the beast's eyes were closed, a low rumble of his breaths passing through his parted snout.

I should try to crawl out into the night and find my way back to the palace where people were probably searching for me. I thought about the hate between the king and Desmire, but Rune awoke.

"Rune." I trembled, reaching my hand up to lightly caress his arm in a soothing manner, one that hopefully showed him I wasn't a threat. I doubted he'd bring me here and hold me like this if he thought I was going to hurt him.

Was he fully an animal now, acting as a predator would? Or was Rune still the dominant species in there, fully in control but the essence of the werewolf core coming out with the full moon?

Rune huffed and turned his head back to where it was before, closing his eyes restfully. I watched him, feeling his deep breaths against my back since we sat against the wall of the cave with me in his lap, his caging arms around me. Obviously he would not be up for letting me leave tonight. Thankfully, I was comfortable against his large furry body despite the situation. I drifted off with his moving chest as he inhaled and exhaled.

I let myself fall asleep, deciding I'd deal with all the new things that occurred tomorrow.

***

A groan woke me up from my deep sleep. I was face to face with Rune's Fae lips.

He was awaking at the same moment, and it took me seconds to gaze down and see that besides the necklace and black trousers, he was bare against my back and still holding me.

"Sapphira?" Rune muttered in confusion, his eyes adjusting to the light beaming in through the cave entrance.

"Uh, hi." I tried to move and at first Rune refused to let me go. Then he realized what was happening and opened his arms with Fae speed.

"What happened?"

I used the cave wall to stand. A bright light made me grimace as I looked toward the blasphemous glare and saw metal bolts connected to the stone wall with broken chains swaying in the breeze of the cave entryway. This was Rune's werewolf cave where he stayed during the full moon. I assumed during the day he was Fae and at night a beast.

"Sapphira." He said my name again, not rising from the wall. I wondered if he could . . . maybe changing back and forth took all his strength.

"We were attacked last night. Some of Verin's soldiers. They kidnapped me, slayed a few of the guards, but were stopped by my dragon friend at the river." The memory of Desmire's roar and fire wall made me shiver. He was so powerful, even without magic.

"You showed up and snarled at everyone. You know, the normal stuff," I teased, hoping to cheer up the quiet rage simmering beneath his features. "You bit a guy's head off with your werewolf teeth, and then carried me here like a ragdoll. Then you . . . uh . . ." Did I tell him he kept me in his arms all night like a protector?

"You caged me in your arms like your favorite teddy bear. And now you're back to you, and it's daylight."

Rune tried to stand. His limbs trembled from the movement and he collapsed against the hard ground with a grunt. I rushed to help him.

"It's no use. I won't have any strength to move till closer to dark." He huffed, and my throat burned, with tears not far behind. It must be awful chained in here for days, then sitting around doing nothing, waiting for it all to be over.

I should leave and let everyone know I was safe, but I couldn't leave him right now. The decision was easier than it should have been as I walked over and plopped down against the wall beside him.

"We've got some time to kill. I think I'm owed a story." I bumped him with my shoulder. We could be alone and simply talk friend to friend in a cave together, as long as I didn't look at him and his naked chest.

Chapter Forty-Two

"A story, huh? Which story?"

I wanted to throw my fist in the air victoriously. Rune was opening up to me.

"I wanna know your story with Nyx. I want to know about your werewolf side. If you weren't in control last night, then it did sort of kidnap me." Rune rested his head against the cave wall.

"When magic was still on this Earth, I was able to control that side of me. It's like we are two beasts sharing one heart. I was able to see what the beast was doing and control him. He knew Nyx was his mate right away, even before I did, and she could control him, too." He chuckled.

"I used to call her my moon. She was the only one my other side liked and would let control him. Now that magic is gone, I've been useless in there. The essence of the wolf is too strong and without my magic, I can't do anything except make sure it doesn't hurt anybody."

"The werewolf side of you is pretty scary. So tall and big. And those teeth." I wanted to peel back his lips and examine those typical Fae elongated canines of his to see if any remained wolf-like.

"Must not have been too scary if you stayed in his arms all night." He didn't say *his* arms, even though technically it was him holding me throughout the night.

"Maybe I've tamed the big bad wolf like the princess did." As soon as the words were out, I wanted to take them back. Nyx was his mate, the werewolf's mate. I was a human who sort of dated his brother.

Rune didn't say anything about my comment, and I was thankful. I looked down at my ruined dress and cringed. I know the rest of me looked as ruined as the torn material covering me.

"After she battled the goblins in the woods, I walked her back to town, not knowing she was the princess. She wasn't ready to leave my side, and I didn't want her to, either. So, we walked around town and the gardens before parting ways, like a normal man and woman getting to know each other."

Except they weren't a normal couple.

"We tried fighting it while Tor courted her for the proposal of marriage, but the pull was too strong. My werewolf essence intensified the mate's draw since it was in the wolf's nature to claim its mate. So, what I felt was magnified than what normal Fae feel. Her essence made her feel love strongly, and she was so smart. She knew what was happening, too. Tor wasn't really interested in marrying her, not like I was. He was doing what was expected of him from our father." His hand moved to the black round gem that rested gentle against his chest.

"Was that hers?"

He continued fidgeting with the necklace. "Days before everything happened, she became frantic, talking about Verin, her father, and how she needed to do something that was dangerous . . . that I needed to trust her. She gave me this the day before magic was lost. We were going to sneak to the priestess and marry that day, but I was called away and she said she had to talk with her parents. She gave this to me before we parted, told me to keep it safe, and remember her. I was fighting against Verin's forces when it happened. I came back as fast as I could to the palace to protect her. She was already in the onyx when I made it back." His hand fisted the gem, the only thing of hers he had.

"Do you know what she did that was dangerous?" I asked, and he shook his head.

"She just kept saying that the darkness was coming, that he knew about her, and she wasn't ready yet." The pain in his voice made my heart ache. I imagined her scribbling in her room. The pain must be imaginable to watch someone you loved be so unhinged. Rune was a protector, and he couldn't have done anything to save her from her onyx fate.

"I think Verin tried to kidnap me because I must be getting close to freeing her." A part of me wished to give him hope that he would be reunited with his love.

"Are you?"

Swallowing hard, I answered with a nod.

"I think so. I've learned a lot about her, and so many things don't make sense. She doesn't seem like the type to lay down and accept the fate of being in onyx while her people suffered. She's also holding something in her hands, like a stone at the end of the necklace. The king is creepy and the queen, I don't know. I wish I could understand what all her random words mean. It has to be her way of talking. And I know you aren't going to like what I have to say, but I broke into Nyx's room. She was reading some weird stuff about Fae cores and tales of a mad scientist."

Rune's hand touched my face to stop my rambling. His touch made me speechless and I didn't feel anything besides his hand on my cheek, a balm to my worrying mind.

"You'll figure it out. You're smarter than you think and a fighter."

The yearning, the draw to touch him was too strong with us this close. He peered into my soul and there was no fear. Like a match when it touched the striker box, our world lit into flames. Our bodies were magnetic, and there was no resistance this time.

I leaned into his space at the same time he crossed into mine, our lips meeting in the middle.

Chapter Forty-Three

I trembled. His scent, his touch . . . everything I'd imagined and more. My life ended and began where his breath mixed with mine. His fingers slipped from my cheek to my neck, pulling me closer. I wasn't close enough. I wasn't nearly close as we needed to be. The fire inside me danced, craving more of his burning touch on my skin. Consuming me, claiming me.

Without parting our lips, I climbed on top of him, my dress pushed up to the tops of my thighs. His free hand ran up them and his pained groan vibrated into my soul. His tongue swept into my parted lips and caressed against the roof of my mouth. I clenched at his possession of my body. There was no part of him I did not want, no piece of him I would not claim. I was whole, forged anew from his kiss.

"You're mine." I growled into his mouth, my unrightful claim barreling into his lungs, his heart.

My hands touched his bare torso, making his fingers grip me tighter. A snarl roared from his chest into my mouth. He was so strong . . . the fighter and werewolf hosted inside one being. My fingers bumped into the necklace, and I was no longer in the cave kissing Rune.

"I'll marry you tomorrow, I promise. Now let me go, you brute." I leaned my head away from his eager lips, needing to go. I had so much to do. I needed to make sure of what I saw. My mate's

kissing was all too easy to fall into and lose myself. We'd have time . . . another time. I hated lying to him, but it had to be done. It was the only way to save us, to save my people. I would sacrifice everything for them and it would not be my end. I would be back.

"After we defeat Verin's forces, you are mine, not my brother's," my love growled into my neck and reluctantly let me go.

"I have always been yours, since I came into this world. More than that Rune, I choose you, not Tor."

Screw it. I turned and gave him one last kiss, pouring out every unspoken word inside me. I believed he would forgive me and I believed in the power of love and our mating bond. The werewolf in him made it more potent. He may end up forgetting me, but his wolf . . . his heart . . . would know mine.

"I'll see you soon." I pushed back from his hard chest and I touched the necklace I had placed around his neck. Safe.

"Soon, wife." Rune smirked, and my heart shattered into tiny pieces.

One day, just not today.

He ran off toward the armory where the guards were choosing their weapons to protect our kingdom from Verin's invading army.

He was already here, though, strutting around like he wasn't the epitome of all evil. My father and mother told me the truth, but more convincing than the truth was the bond, the connection between us. My father was strong and determined, a true warrior and protector, like Rune. Like mother like daughter, I guess. Both fell for the warrior brother they shouldn't have.

I ran toward the room where I told my parents to wait for me. Celestine had warned them this was going to happen, though it didn't stop the tears from flowing down my mother's face when I confirmed what she already knew.

It was going to be hard, but we had to do it for our world.

"There you are, my little gem. I've been so worried about you." My focus shifted to the little box in the king's hand, then back at his golden eyes.

One day, just not today.

"Holy fuck." My body flung back from Rune's kiss swollen lips and the necklace.

Stunned, Rune watched me, as I panicked.

"Did you see that?" My fingers touched my lips, feeling the wetness from Rune's kiss and then to my head. Had I been far more injured than I thought? Was this all a dream?

"I didn't see anything. Sapphira?" Rune tried to move, the strain on his face visible as he crawled toward me in pain.

"I saw you and the king. It was like I was in her head right before everything happened. I saw you two promising to marry each other, that you were going to battle Verin's army, and your final kiss before you never saw each other again." Rune's face paled as he remembered the moment.

"How?" he managed to grunt as he finished his last stretch toward me, his hand reaching to touch my face again.

"I don't know. I—"

Except I did know. I think I finally knew the answers, and my stomach began to roll.

"Is . . . is it possible to have two . . . two mates?" I stammered; it couldn't be.

"Not that I know of. Sapphira, tell me," he pleaded, and my tears fell.

"I have to go. I have to get back to the palace and the queen, but I promise I will be back. I have to go." I scrambled away.

"Sapphira!" Rune's voice raised as I stood.

"I will be back before tonight. I promise, Rune."

Rune didn't like it, but he could barely move and I had a seer to visit.

Chapter Forty-Four

Rune's isolation cave was not far from the palace. But I ran in my torn dress to Celestine's cave where I knew she waited for me. It was odd seeing her and her wooded home in the daylight. Tea was waiting for me, and this time I kicked it over.

"I don't want your bullshit tea. What have you been doing to me? Why am I seeing all these things? Visions, memories, whatever the hell they are." I paced while she grinned, enjoying my fluster.

"I've been making a batch of tea for twenty years with opal inside and a tiniest bit of my blood. Opal increases mystical and psychic visions. You are seeing what you needed to see, and since you have seen it, you are ready." Celestine floated to where I stood. She observed me as she walked around my body like an inspector.

"It can't be."

"But it is, my dear. It is." Her fingers pushed back some of the hair in my face tenderly.

"Why would the queen do that? Marry him?" My mind tried to process what I was learning.

"She didn't know at first when they wed, since the evil king has always been covered, but then it was too late. She's continued to keep the peace until another way to defeat him presented itself." Celestine's face fell at this admission of truth. The poor queen.

"I can't believe it. Ugh . . . yes, I really can."

I wished I hadn't knocked the tea over. It made me calmer and soothed my overthinking mind. My thoughts raced too fast to focus.

"Your time has run out, you know this, yes?" Celestine's warm hands wrapped around mine.

I nodded. Whether I was ready or not, it was time to decide. Right here, right now. After I left this cave, there would be no going back.

"Save Tor. Go tonight and unlock the secrets in the onyx. Get her out of that tomb." She shook my hands slightly with every word, driving her serious tone home with every movement.

"Can you tell me the downside to this? I know there is one. Life works in balances." It was something I'd learned long ago. Without the bad, there was no good. Everything had an opposite.

"You will be exposing the Fae realm to the Dramens, and they will start a war with our kind. Saving them means a destiny of suffering and loss. However, you will gain so much more in the end . . . a better world for everyone, human and Fae alike. You listen to me, dear. Hear me good. You have the strength of all the creatures of this Earth. We are all with you, and you will never be alone in this fate."

I knew her demand of saving Tor and the princess were too good to be true. To save them meant war, death, and pain. It all rested on my shoulders.

"I'm not ready for this." I shook my head. I wished I knew someone else who could take my place and go work miracles with the fate of many people tied to them.

"You are. You already know you are. Stop fighting your destiny." She willed me to see it, to feel what I knew.

"How would I even get to the Iron City? No doubt those Dramens are almost there with him." I couldn't believe I was really doing this, taking a leap of faith.

"I think a certain dragon would be happy to help you get there quickly." The seer released my hand, while one of her pets landed on her shoulder with a purr.

"I must be going mad."

"All the best people are a little mad. It's what sets us apart from the crowd." Celestine winked and walked around her fire and poured herself some tea.

Weeks ago, all I wanted was to be part of a crowd, a community where I was safe, and live out my days in peace. Instead I was some wannabe warrior who was about to ask a dragon to fly me to where the king and queen of the Dramens sat on their bone thrones. I'd have to face an army of feral humans to save Tor. By myself.

Then, if I survived, I'd be letting the rest of the human world know the Fae and mystical creatures were real. I had many theories about the onyx tomb, but that would have to wait until I came back. *If* I came back. There were more important matters right now.

"What should I do if I see the king?" Unpleasant chills ran down my spine at the thought of the royal Fae.

"He pretends, so you will pretend for now." She shrugged.

"Does he know about me? What I'm supposed to do?"

"He knows now. Seeing Desmire connected everything he was suspicious about. You don't have much time to get your plan ready, my dear. You need to go."

"What about the rest of it. Is it true?"

I knew my suspicions about King Lachan were correct. It was so obvious now. The other things my nagging mind tried to reveal were too much to handle. I swallowed a thick lump in my throat as I took one step back toward the exit.

"You'll figure it out soon enough."

OK. For now, I had to somehow save Tor from the Dramen's Iron City and get Nyx out of the onyx tomb.

And stay the hell away from King Verin, who strutted around the palace as their King Lachan.

Chapter Forty-Five

The guards alerted everyone I was back and alive. Dris and Emrys waited for me, as well as the queen and king.

I plastered a mask of relief on my face as I ran to embrace them, instead of concentrating on the internal recoil upon seeing the king's golden gaze settle on me.

"Are you OK? Holy hell, we saw a werewolf carry you off into the woods." Dris sobbed so hard, her shoulders shook as she hugged me. Emrys's normally grinning face was serious and grim. His hair and clothes looked like he hadn't been able to sleep. Guilt for not coming here first bloomed in my belly.

The queen wasn't looking at me, and the king noticed his wife's aloof behavior with suspicion.

"My wife is tired. Now that we see you are in good health, we will retreat to our beds. We are very happy to see you safe and sound, little gem." The king placed his hand on the queen's elbow and steered her off toward the inside of the palace.

The poor queen, married to her enemy, couldn't fight back because she'd given everything she had to save her daughter.

"What happened?" Emrys questioned me softly, and I motioned for them to follow me to my small quarters.

They looked at each other and nodded, staying close to me as we walked to my room. The room was slightly cramped once we all piled in and had the door closed behind me, but it would have to do for now.

"Rune was the werewolf. I am fine. But I found out some heavy stuff and have a crazy plan to start working on."

"I'm in," Emrys announced, his hands going into his pockets.

"I haven't even said anything yet."

"Doesn't matter. Whatever you're up to, I'm in." He shrugged.

"Sapphira. What did you find out?" she asked.

"King Lachan is Verin. That's why there has been peace between the two kingdoms in the past twenty years. He has everything he wants. No need to fight when you are the ruler of both. I don't know if he was always named Verin and changed it to Lachan or vice versa. I don't know if he wanted me dead or a prisoner, but he had his men attack the party. He invited me and knew I'd be there. He knows that I'm trying to break the princess out of the onyx tomb. She could change what he unleashed in this world, and he wants her to stay there. Hence I need to go."

Dris sat down on my bed, like her legs couldn't hold the weight from my words. Emrys cursed and ran his hands over his face, having trouble dealing with the information.

"You mentioned a plan?" Dris spoke softly, accepting what I said and moving on to the next part of our little meeting.

I said with conviction, "I'm going to fly to the Iron City to save Tor, and then open that onyx tomb. I believe Tor has the final piece to this large puzzle, and he needs to be freed from those evil creatures. Verin will try to stop me from all of this so that's why I'm leaving tonight." I nodded to myself, believing my own words, and knowing I still had so much to do.

"Fly?" Emrys asked. The excited smile on his face indicated he was confused and wanted a confirmation of his thoughts.

I grinned with him as I spoke clearly. "I'm going to convince my dragon friend to take me. We'll be there in a few hours and hopefully out of there in no time. One thing you must know before any of this goes further, Emrys. Doing this will be exposing the Fae realm to the humans, and there is no coming back. There will be war, eventually." It was a large burden to carry, but Emrys didn't even blink before agreeing he wanted to help with the plan.

"I'm in, too." My owl friend spoke with a newfound boldness as a warrior, not a librarian.

"Can you fight?" I didn't want to insult her, but she was always in the library, so my question wasn't unreasonable.

She gave me a look that promised I would pay for asking. "I can hold my own, and you will fail with this plan if you do not have knowledge. You need me to succeed. Books are weapons, my dearest friend, and I've read a lot of books."

"Damn right you have. OK. I need to get out of this dress and then we plan. Meet in the dark library?"

They both nodded.

"I'm glad you're OK." Dris hugged me again as they walked toward the door and left me alone with my thoughts.

The bath I took was quick, and I changed into a pair of leggings I knew wouldn't hinder any movements and a long-sleeved tunic that stopped just below my waist.

Once dressed, I didn't head down to the dark library. There was one more thing I needed to do . . . something I hadn't spoken aloud yet. There was another fear throbbing in my chest.

I picked up one of Princess Nyx's books and read.

Books were a weapon, and she'd figured out how to even the scales against Verin from them. Now it was my turn.

Chapter Forty-Six

"Sapphira! Perfect timing. I knew there was something in here about the city where Tor is headed with those humans."

My friend twisted a book she'd been reading toward my direction. Emrys had let me into the dark library where we could talk freely without someone hearing our conversation. Dris's head popped up to look at me with a victorious grin on her face, then it faded. "Are you OK? You look sick."

I nodded. I'd pieced together another clue I wasn't ready for, and neither were they. I needed Tor; only he could help me right now. He knew the truth or at least suspected it.

Dris could see through my bullshit nod, knowing very well that I was not OK. I knew she would let me be, and that she knew I'd tell her when I was ready.

"What did you find?" I stopped at the dusty table and looked at the pages within the book she'd gotten excited over.

"It's a book written by a Fae who was captured and escaped the Iron City. He talks in great detail about the wall made of iron spikes with human heads impaled on them. And the large castle in the middle has the metal on it lit up like a beacon of the sun. He also talked about their holding cells for the auction. He was meticulous in counting steps and listening to his surroundings. It's how he escaped. He attacked one of the guards, donned his outfit, and followed the steps and turns out of the gate. Other than that, I haven't found any tellings about those awful humans since. It seems like our people and yours have stayed far away from each other."

Not for long. Soon the Fae would have the Dramens at their door and Verin's army to contend with.

"Good stuff. I'll take a look at it on our way. Emrys, you may want to read up, too. You probably could sneak in and get Tor easier than I could."

The spider nodded and walked over to the chair next to Dris. "What now?" Dris asked.

"I go talk to a dragon, we gather weapons, and go. It will only take us a few hours flying to get there instead of the three weeks on foot. We slip in while it's dark, fight anyone who gets in our way, don't get caught or killed, grab Tor, and get the hell out of there."

It was the easiest plan I could think of, and hopefully the most effective. Emrys was going to find me a way in, Dris was my walking, talking library, and Desmire was our ride and possible distraction.

"Emrys, after you've finished getting an idea of the layout, do you think you guys could swipe some weapons from the armory? I don't think they'd let us take a whole bunch, especially now that Verin knows who I am and what I'm after."

Emrys nodded. He and Dris still looked a little shocked when I said Verin's name so casually in association to the king. He'd been pretending to be someone good and kind all the while being truly evil on the inside.

"Any particular weapon of choice for you?" Emrys asked, and I thought about what I'd want in my hands if it came to battle with a Dramen.

"Hatchets."

"I'll meet you guys by the waterfall in an hour. Bring the book and anything else you think we need. We need to be quick and as stealthy as we can."

Before I turned to leave the room, I remembered the gun the Dramen had shot Tor with. "They have guns. Is there any kind of armor that could protect us from bullets?" My confidence wavered with the thoughts of bullets aimed for my friends and myself. I wasn't as fast as Fae or as agile. I couldn't outrun them.

"I'll see what I can find," Dris answered, as she pulled the spines of books out to look at the cover, then pushed them back in.

I wanted to hug them both so hard for doing this, for standing up and fighting, but there would be time for that later. We needed to get moving.

As soon as I left the libraries, I saw Najen. "My king requests that you have an escort around Crysia, just in case Verin's soldiers come after you again."

I couldn't fault Najen for believing his king. Najen wanted to protect me from incoming danger, but he also didn't know where the true danger lurked.

I would figure out on my walk to the Hallowstags if I would try to escape Najen before talking to Desmire or let him hear everything about his king and my plans.

"Are you doing OK? Last night was quite an event for you." Najen tried to lighten the mood.

"I'm doing OK. I'm a tough girl. Those soldiers are lucky I didn't have my hatchets with me." I winked and he chuckled.

We walked together in silence, both of us caught up in our own thoughts. I was still unsure if I should make a run for it and escape my friend, or if I should let him in on my plans.

"You're dismissed, Najen. I'll take over as Sapphira's escort from here."

Rune had made the decision for me. Najen's head bowed in understanding and left without a word. His general had given him a command.

Rune had found a shirt to cover his broad chest and the outline of Nyx's necklace showed beneath the soft black material. A shiver ran down my body remembering the memory that necklace made me see.

"You look like you are in pain."

Rune stood tall but his face was coated in a sheen of sweat. "It's not without effort to get here. I'll be fine. Tell me everything." His teeth clenched as he took another step toward me, barely leaving a foot between us.

Chapter Forty-Seven

"Verin is King Lachan. He's been hiding in plain sight and happy to rule Crysia and his badlands in disguise. He knows who I am and what I'm after and will try to stop me. Tor is the final puzzle piece I need to open the onyx tomb, so I'm going to rescue him tonight."

He didn't exactly seem shocked by my admission.

"I'm coming with you."

I was afraid he was going to say that, but before I could protest, his fingers were against my lips. Once his touch soothed me, I knew I couldn't rescue Tor without him. I needed him.

"I'll be fine, and something tells me my werewolf side wouldn't mind assisting in this little rescue." His eyebrow arched high, daring me to question his statement.

I didn't.

"Tell me what this is. When I look at you, I feel pain and longing. I know my mate is alive. She's locked in that cursed rock. When I touch you, when I feel your lips, I feel an unyielding force in my soul. I've never known anyone to have two mates, but that's what this feels like. I'm confused and feel guilty like I'm betraying her." The fingers on my lips moved to cup my cheek, and I wanted so badly to lean into them, to close my eyes and feel his warmth, his comfort, and his feelings from the single touch.

A shudder racked my body. My shoulders shook with the threat of tears. Instead, I took a deep, shaky breath to stop the tears. "What were the princess's powers?" I knew he wouldn't like that I asked a question instead of answering his.

His hand dropped and I instantly grew cold from the lack of his warm touch against me.

"Do you not feel this, too?" His words were so soft, I barely heard them.

I did. It was like suffocating, keeping those emotions inside. I wanted to release my feeling, my thoughts. But the timing wasn't right.

"Save Tor, break the onyx, and then we can figure this out. Together."

I hoped my words rang true. Rune was not happy about my answer but he nodded.

"Do you remember her powers before?" I asked again.

"I don't remember." I wasn't surprised. Tor was the only person who knew, and his answer was the key to breaking her out of the tomb.

The ground shook and a roar echoed throughout the forest. Rune maintained his stance at the approach of the large, dark dragon who stomped toward us. A growl escaped his massive snout.

"Desmire. My friend. I need you." I walked up to him and said to Rune who was behind me with his body positioned to fight, "He won't hurt me."

"To break the onyx, I need to rescue Tor from the Dramens in the human realm in the Iron City. I fear going by horseback will result in his death. I need your strength, your heart, and your wings. Fly with me, Desmire. Protect me and my friends. Fight with me and help me save the world from the hands of evil." I reached out and pressed a hand to the broad scales across his chest, where his heart beat thunderously beneath my touch.

I waited for some sign from him. I knew he would help. He'd chosen me, he protected me, and he exposed himself to the Fae king to do so.

"We're risking much, but I believe there is much more to gain." My last line defended my choice of possibly throwing this realm into war with the humans. I heard the crunch of leaves behind me, then a hand gently rested on my shoulder. My head tilted back to look at the general, who held such a vast ocean of emotions in his gaze. It was a rare sight to see him so open, so freeing, and yet I knew he might hate me in the end, even if I still cared deeply.

Rescue Tor, open the onyx, then figure it out.

I repeated the phrase in my head a few times. A huff reverberated from the dragon beneath my fingers, and I dropped my hand before taking a few steps back, giving Desmire space.

"You could have been a general with that speech," Rune whispered in my ear, and for a few seconds I closed my eyes and basked in the warm breath that passed from his lips to my neck, tickling the curls free of my bun.

The dragon huffed again in a very human-like manner, then brought his big snout to my feet, nudging me gently. I smiled and pet the scales of his head. "Thank you, my friend, my dragon protector. Make sure to stretch those big bones of yours because you will be carrying a few of us, including this brute of a Fae." I gestured to Rune who only rolled his eyes.

The dragon lifted his head in acceptance. I swore I saw the beast roll his eyes, too.

I had managed to get Desmire on my side to rescue Tor. Now we needed to haul ass before the king stopped me.

Chapter Forty-Eight

"If Verin knows you are going to break the princess out of the tomb, I doubt he's going to let you leave tonight. Najen was not sent under my orders. The king is watching you. If you show up to get supplies, you will be put under house arrest for some bullshit so you can't leave."

Rune had a good point. I wasn't as stealthy as Emrys, and Rune wasn't in the shape to run back and forth.

"If you're suddenly out of ideas, I suggest we take the dragon and pick them up. It has the element of surprise and I know none of my army can fight him off at this time. Not even Verin could fight him without magic."

I wanted to hug him. "Such a smart troublemaker you are!" I enjoyed this bantering between us . . . not enemies, not friends, but something different.

Desmire must have heard us because he lowered his body as close to the ground as he could beside me, lowering the webbed points along his back so we could climb on without being stabbed.

A little squeal may have bubbled up from my chest eagerly. No fear trembled inside my body as I climbed on top of the dragon and settled against the base of his neck. Rune grunted slightly with the struggling effort it took for him to put one leg over the beast to straddle behind me.

"This is not going to be a comfortable flight," Rune mumbled, and I laughed. Who knew the cure to carrying the weight of the world was sitting on the back of a dragon?

"Grouchy old man," I teased. As Desmire rose to his feet, our bodies swayed from side to side. Rune's strong arms wrapped around my waist, keeping himself rooted to me as I grabbed onto the two webbed points near my hands like reins on a horse.

Tension radiated from Rune, making me squeeze my legs a little tighter against the dragon. He had a retort to my old-man tease, one that would surely bring heat to my cheeks. I knew it was hanging on the tip of his tongue as he fought back saying something that couldn't be undone.

Wait. Just wait.

I willed him to keep it at bay, to be patient until we got Nyx out of that onyx.

Desmire opened his vast black wings, which had a tiny hint of gold in the membrane, and stretched wide. That was all the warning we got before he shot up into the clouds.

My grip was tight, and Rune was plastered to my back, his strong legs holding him in place behind me. My stomach dropped, and the weight of the wind was heavy, but my smile defied gravity. Once Desmire leveled out, his wings flapped in long strokes through the air. I lifted my hands off his spine and held them out wide, laughing and hollering at the sky.

I was flying.

I was flying on a damned dragon.

"You are incredible," Rune said against my neck, and I pressed my head against his gently, feeling the connection between us in this moment, feeling his tiger's eye core giving me the strength to be brave.

It took two minutes to get to the open gardens near the library where guards started shouting and moving with their swords toward us as Desmire opened his mouth wide. Fire shot out at their feet to back them up but not turn them to ash.

Dris and Emrys burst through the door on the other side of the garden with their hands full. Emrys had a large bag with weapons in it, and Dris carried her two books with shimmering arms. They moved with Fae speed toward us.

"Don't let them leave." The king's bellow reached our ears as Emrys helped Dris climb onto Desmire behind the general, then threw one leg over the beast himself, the heavy bag hanging in his hand.

Verin's hate surrounded him . . . for me and for the dragon. Desmire snarled at the king's presence, blasting fire in his direction. Suddenly, Desmire closed his snout when the queen took a step beside the king. She wore a light blue gown with off-the-shoulder sleeves and white diamonds dripping from the tight bodice down to the grass. She screamed with tears in her eyes and fell like she was in pain.

The beast beneath us shuddered in pain. But with my friends on his back, and Verin distracted by the queen, it was our only time to escape.

"We must go, Desmire. We will come back for her, and I will make all this right," I vowed, and hesitating, he spread his wings and took off. The farther we got from the palace, the more pain I sensed in my dragon's heart. He and the queen loved each other, which confirmed some suspicions I had.

"The librarian said you needed to see this." Rune tapped my shoulder and handed me a book.

The wind was merciless against the pages, though I managed to block most of the heavy gusts behind Desmire's neck. It had a purple cover and a tassel wrapped on a hook with a little white gem in the middle. I gasped. It was the queen's journal, one she had written before she married Verin and had the princess.

He made me feel so safe and cherished. He didn't want me for my power or title as queen. He wanted me for me.

I wasn't in love with his brother. That man was cold and deceiving, only working toward his own personal agenda in courting me. One man I had to be with for the courts to hold peace between our people.

Why I couldn't do the same thing with his brother was absurd, but their father knew Lachan would be a more wicked king than my love. My mate.

I despised the sneaking around with the warrior, who's eyes of smoke consumed me. It was the only way to be together.

For I was not willing to let him go, to give up love for power.

My mate was power, my match in every way.

For what would better suit a core of diamond than that of a dragon and an onyx core, beating in one body.

My mate. My Desmire.

Chapter Forty-Nine

The portal to the human realm in the red tree would not be able to handle the size of a dragon. Thankfully Dris knew of another way, flying for half an hour to the sea, then we'd turn back toward the middle of the continent.

This time, I saw what a Fae portal looked like . . . shimmery, like a heavy rain falling.

We stopped just after the crossing through the cave that led to the ocean, collecting our bearings. Rune and Emrys went through the bag of armor and weapons, while Desmire sat near the cliff overlooking the water and the slowly descending sun.

With the queen's journal in my hand, I walked up to Dris and hugged her tightly.

"Did you show them the journal entry you marked for me?" I whispered, hoping it was low enough to be just between us.

"No," she replied and the tension in my shoulders released.

Desmire and the queen had been in love—mates. My dragon friend was *the* Desmire.

Dris and I knew who the onyx core belonged to now, but what she didn't know was the little details in the memory I'd had from the princess before she was put in the tomb. She had said "father" and then "king" separately. She knew Verin was not her actual dad.

Desmire was her father. The queen married Verin, for whatever reason, but she was no more than a wife in name to him. Her heart and soul belonged to the dragon who looked at the water clashing against the rocks.

"But the records book said Desmire died, and he didn't have a core of onyx." I pulled back, whispering so the boys wouldn't hear.

"I think someone covered up the truth and replaced reality with their own agenda, hiding something larger than we knew. He was a Fae, and with magic gone, stuck as a dragon." Dris's face was grim and pale.

Someone didn't want us to know about Desmire, about his cores, or that he was even alive. Immediately I thought this was Verin's handiwork, but after reading just that one entry in the queen's journal and seeing them together, I wondered if she was the one who covered it up to protect him and allowed Verin to think that her love—his brother—was dead.

So many secrets, so many lies.

"That's probably why he's been helping you so much. He knows you're the only hope he has at getting his daughter out of the onyx . . . the onyx he placed her in to save her." Dris finally understood that the princess was Desmire's, not Verin's, daughter. A deep breath released from her lungs, and she sounded like how I felt, blown away and tired from this life of secrecy.

The constant revelations and surprises cast my way were exhausting. I wanted to sleep, and just pretend it wasn't any of my business. Only it was, I stood at the heart of this whole thing, and I'd come too far to turn back.

"Ladies," Emrys called to us with his grin on his face.

"Are you guys becoming the best of friends yet? Male bonding over sharp weapons?" I put on a mask of contentment, not ready to reveal what I'd learned. Rune's look was comical. He clearly thought I was crazy for bringing these two here.

A human, a werewolf, a librarian, and a spider walk into an Iron City. Sounded like the makings of another joke, if it wasn't real life and dangerous as hell.

"What do we have?" Instead of chuckling like I wanted to, my focus was on the bag of weapons and armor Emrys had managed to swipe before our departure.

Four swords, two smaller sized bows and full quivers, four daggers, and three hatchets.

"I can't believe you actually found the diamond armor." Dris gasped at the thin material, which looked like a white shirt but shimmered in the sunlight.

"He stole it from the locked and guarded room in the bottom of the palace," Rune grumbled, not happy that this goat Fae was able to break into something that he wasn't supposed to.

"All for a good cause. I get the hatchets; you guys can divvy up the rest." I reached to grab the little axes and touched the armor on my way. It felt soft and light in my hands, despite the diamonds Dris said were weaved in it.

"It's as hard as diamonds and will stop a bullet." Dris answered the question inside my head. The queen most likely made it for her warriors for past battles.

"You and Dris will wear them. I only could get two before more guards came." Emrys reached down to grab the two tunics and gave them to us. The material was smooth as silk, and I managed to put it on with ease. The sleeves stopped at my shoulders, so it only covered the torso, protecting the most important organs.

"Will you guys be OK?" I didn't like using this armor while leaving them exposed, but both of the men ignored me.

"If anyone needs to take a piss, or whatever, we're leaving in five minutes." Rune commanded us and I raised my eyebrow at him. This was my mission and he was already taking over being general.

While the others were talking about weapons and figuring out how their skill would be most useful, I walked over to Desmire. My heart ached for him. The princess's memory barreled into my thoughts again. She had said like mother like daughter, both destined to marry one brother but fell in love with the other brother instead. Tor was no Verin, though. He was gentle, kind, and dependable.

Desmire's head shifted slightly at my approach, but he didn't move. The water and sky were beautiful. Our world was vast and unique, yet damaged in many ways . . . ways I hoped we could build on and make beautiful again.

The smell of the salty air calmed me and reminded me of the silence in a forest before the storm. "I've never seen the ocean before." I rested a comforting hand on the side of the dragon. "Tor and Mariam would tell me stories about this great body of water, untamed and free. It's every bit as beautiful as I imagined it would be."

He didn't move, but I understood the agreement in his energy. We stared at the water for a silent minute before I said, "I'm sorry you've lost so much. I'm going to help you get it all back and defeat him." Another vow, another job for me to do once Tor and Nyx were free. His smoky eyes filled with sadness. He saw into my soul, my very being. He knew I meant what I'd said.

"You ready for this?" I asked, while bumping my shoulder into his just as my crew walked up to the cliff's edge. Everyone took in the sight of the sun above the deep blue water of the ocean, the sound of the crashing waves, and the smell of the salty air like it was the last time they might ever see it.

I hoped and prayed to whatever higher beings who watched over us that we would see this sight again and we would all come back together.

Desmire released a mighty roar that shook the Earth.

"We're coming, Tor. We're coming," I whispered just as a callused, strong hand wrapped around mine.

Chapter Fifty

"My ass hurts. We need a saddle for that dragon next time we go on a big adventure." Emrys rubbed his backside and I knew Rune was annoyed with the spider. Those two hadn't warmed up to each other during our trip to the Iron City.

Desmire had kept us high in the clouds, staying out of sight in case any Dramens happened to look up. Dris had fallen asleep against Rune's back while Emrys used his arms to cage her in from falling off the flying dragon. Despite knowing I shouldn't, I rested my body against Rune's chest while I read about the Iron City from a Fae's escape. I memorized every word.

"Sundown is soon." Rune's voice sounded pained.

"Do you need to go?"

"No." His clenched his teeth.

There was no time to not trust him. He had been dealing with this all his life. If he said he would be fine, then he would be.

"I can't believe they built all that without power." Dris was wide awake now as we stayed low on top of an old skyscraper.

The Iron City had been built next to what had been a big metropolitan city before the apocalypse. They'd taken over every crevice of the place, using up its resources, and reusing materials found in buildings to make their own. The top of the iron palace gleamed in the setting sun. There were no places to hide out here . . . no trees or mountains . . . just the husks of skyscrapers.

It was once called Tornado Alley. It was barren and flat and in the middle of the continent where all four corners of the Dramen territories came together. The city was a terror to look upon even from here. I really didn't want to go there. Flashbacks of the Dramen's attack on my community made my hands tremble. I was afraid I was going to freeze or be taken by them. The fear tried to beat me down, and I couldn't let it. I rose to my feet and quickly strolled to the pacing general.

"I need you to do something for me." He stopped wearing a path in the roof of the building and looked at me with his complete focus, despite the strain I knew he was in.

"Don't let them take me." My voice cracked, and my body shivered.

"I won't." His words were a promise, but I was still scared. The Dramens world and Crysia were not safe, until we completed our mission. The princess was the bridge between the two worlds. She was powerful, and somehow, she was going to reverse what had been done. Verin was scared of his niece, so he also believed in the legend that she would defeat him someday.

Hands touched my shoulders. "I promise I won't let them take you." Rune leaned down toward my face, his vow caressing me, like it could attach itself to my skin.

Rune's body moved closer, breathing in my air. "This can't be real," he muttered softly, his head slowly descending toward me, or to be more specific, toward my mouth.

But it was real, this thing, this living, breathing force between us.

"Sun's almost down. We need to gear up." I cleared my dry throat and took a step back, out of Rune's reach.

The hurt in his eyes killed me. He didn't know how to decipher his emotions, but he knew he cared for me. I sensed it in his touch, in the air around him. I was something to him, but he had a mate. He'd known that intense connection, the other half of his soul.

Only one more day, then we'd get this all sorted out and—

Before I could finish my thoughts, Rune's arms were wrapped around me, holding me flush against his body. His lips clashed against mine, and every thought I'd been having vanished. My eyes widened, staring into his determined gaze as his lips pressed against mine. His arms moved to my back just in time to hold me to his chest as my legs wobbled, then gave out. My whimper echoed against his mouth as I threw myself into the man who consumed my heart with every swipe of his tongue against mine.

"I don't know what is happening, but whatever comes, I won't let you go," he said.

I shook my head, attempting to push away from his warmth, but his arms were locked around me. "You're not mine, and I'm not yours." It hurt me to say it when everything in me said it wasn't true.

"My heart . . . my werewolf thinks differently." His lips were back on mine, and I was close, so very damn close from disclosing my suspicions of the dangerous truth.

"Rune." I whispered a plea. My fingers gripped the black shirt that covered his thick arms.

"Hey, guys." Emrys cleared his throat and Rune growled. His grip stayed on my back, giving me just enough space to turn my head to look at the spider and librarian who averted their gazes. I managed to untangle myself and walked to the bag of weapons.

"Darkness is upon us." Dris pointed toward the sun, which had almost completely set beyond the flat planes of land behind us. Torches of the palace walls were lit, and the Iron City became the perfect beacon to attack.

"Oh, shit," Emrys said, and reached over to Dris, pulling her behind him as a barrier. He looked behind me at the general.

Rune bellowed a pain-riddled roar as his flesh burst and fur grew out from the rips in his skin. The echo of bones breaking and growing bounced off the city's towers around us. It was horrifying to watch. The man who, moments ago declared things he shouldn't have, was being ripped apart and made into something tall and wild. The beast snarled at the dragon resting on the roof ten yards away, who had both eyes narrowed on the werewolf.

It was time to see if Rune's gut feelings about the werewolf listening to me were based on truth.

Chapter Fifty-One

Seeing Rune's werewolf side was as frightening as it was the first time I saw him. He reached nearly ten feet, had black fur, and sharp white teeth. I wasn't afraid of him, although he looked scary, and I knew what those teeth could do.

Dris gasped and hid behind Emrys with her owl eyes peeking over his shoulder at Rune. The werewolf growled, his muzzle lifting to show a dangerous grin in their direction.

"Rune." I took a step toward the beast. His head swiftly turned as he took a big step on two legs toward me. His massive furry muscles flexed with the movement. He didn't blink as he stared at my face.

My heart beat wildly. "Will you follow me? Protect me and my friends? Will you go into the city with me and help me end all this?" His large wolf-like feet inched closer to me.

"Sapphira, be careful," Dris said.

He was beautiful, in a very savage way, and the raw connection between us was still there . . . even now. Suddenly his large arm and claw-tipped hand shot out and grabbed me by the back of the neck. His grip was strong and hurt slightly. Desmire growled, and I heard the sound of a sword being pulled from the hilt. I motioned behind me for Emrys to lower his weapon. I wasn't in danger, even now with the werewolf's grasp around my neck.

"Will you help me?" I breathed, his head leaning down, looking at me eye to eye, like he was trying to see inside me. My heart thumped in my chest and my breaths became labored with his closeness. It wasn't fear but something else.

The werewolf's eyes closed, then he brought his forehead to rest against mine. I started to cry. Rune was right. I wanted to hold onto this moment of the werewolf accepting me. A whoosh of breath sounded off behind me and I turned to look at my companions. Their postures were still taut and worrisome. But I hadn't been eaten, and it was obvious from Rune's head still resting against mine that he was going to help.

"Thank you, Rune." I reached up and kissed the side of his muzzle before trying to step away. His massive, furry arms wrapped around me tighter, bringing me flush against his pecs.

"OK, you big brute. You've hugged your teddy bear, now let me go so we can kick some ass and rescue a boy in distress." I patted his arms and squiggled free from his hold. Dris coughed up a laugh of relief.

Rune sniffed the air and walked toward Desmire.

"Did you guys have any thought on where we could enter the palace initially? After reading the story of the Fae who got away, I think the queen's balcony would be a good place." I walked over to our bag of weapons and strapped myself with the sharp objects. I'd already been wearing the diamond armor, which felt light as a scarf on my body, but it was not a very subtle color. When we were at the cliff, I'd put the armor underneath my tunic to help camouflage me. Dris had sneaked off with me and done the same without the gazes of the men on our naked torsos.

"I think that is a wise plan," Dris said, buckling her sword belt onto her hip, then tucking a dagger into her boot.

"I'll sneak in first and find out if he's in the holding cell. If I can get him out, I will, and if I don't come back to the balcony in five minutes, then you come in because I ran into trouble." Emrys grabbed a bow and quiver and nestled a sword across his back and a dagger at his hips.

"Desmire can stay out of sight in the dark, and he has fire power if we need it." While I hoped this rescue went smoothly, I knew it wasn't going to be as easy as we wished.

"How will we communicate with each other?" Dris asked, and it was a good question. I looked at Emrys for ideas. If this was the older days, humans had devices like phones. But those didn't work in our present.

"You both know the Iron City's layout from the book. We'll meet in the trophy room. Chances are they will be busy in other parts and not look there for any intruders there."

Emrys just had to pick that room for our meeting. Both Dris and I grimaced at the mention of the trophy room. The book had described the horrors on display in there.

"Go there and hide if you can until we are together. Hopefully I'll find Prince Torin and we'll escape the same way I came in. If not, then you'll see me without him there."

It made sense. Rune sniffed the door to the tower beneath us, his claws raking against the metal with ear-cringing sounds. He grasped onto the handle and ripped it off the hinge. Two gunshots echoed in the still air of the city, and my heart experienced every bullet like it was mine getting hit instead of Rune's.

Chapter Fifty-Two

My scream echoed far into the Iron City. Moving faster than my mind had the option to react, I grabbed my hatchet and threw it with all my strength into the chest of the Dramen.

"Rune!" I sobbed, stumbling toward the werewolf who was crouched on the ground, panting. My hands reached out, touching his chest and muzzle. "Oh God, your arm." My hand went to the wound, which was a little bleeding hole in his arm. The bullet was probably still in there and we needed to get it out. However, the bullet began to move out of the torn flesh, like his body was rejecting the metal and pushing it out.

"Rune?" I watched in awe as the bleeding slowed, and his heavy pants turned to more calming, even breaths. I wanted to leap, cry, and fight all at the same time.

"Let's go get those bastards!" I leaned in and pressed my forehead to his snout. I then stood to check out what weapons the Dramen had on him besides a gun.

Rune was OK. Rune was not dead. I repeated these sentences as a silent rage settled in my blood. I wanted to hurt, kill, and maim. I wanted to show no mercy like they have done to all of mankind. Murdering and taking what they wanted. Dramens were past redeeming, and they almost killed my—

No.

I focused on that killing song humming beneath my skin. My hands gripped the hatchet buried in the Dramen's chest and pulled. Even the sound of metal scraping against flesh and bone did not deter me from the desire for revenge. Revenge for everyone.

"Emrys, do you think you can shoot this thing?" I picked up the gun and held it out. It was a pistol, but I didn't know how it worked. Most people in this era didn't except the Dramens, who hoarded them like a god they worshiped.

"I'll try." He accepted the gun and tinkered, inspecting the anatomy to figure out how it worked.

"Dangerous." He sniffed it and shook his head while muttering to himself.

"I think we should take its clothes, too. Might give Emrys more of an edge in the castle." Dris walked forward with a pressed mouth. She held no kindness in her expression as she looked down at the dead Dramen, then to Rune.

"I'm glad you're OK." She offered kindness to the werewolf and he slightly nodded in acknowledgment.

"How is it possible?" she asked me, wanting the truth that she'd seen between the general and me.

"Debaru," I whispered, almost afraid to say it aloud. I had no doubts now on what I knew to be true. Dris saw it, felt it. As did I. She nodded, knowing it wasn't the time or place to discuss this huge secret that had unraveled at our feet. But I swear the owl Fae's face turned into that of a warrior. She looked confident and mighty, like she might very well use that sword at her hip and do it with honor.

We began de-robing the dead man and tossing the discarded clothes in the direction of Emrys. None of us knew if there were more Dramens around, or if some heard the gunshot and were coming, so we tried to move from our location as quickly as possible.

"These smell awful." Emrys scrunched up his nose as he changed into his new attire.

"Good! Then they won't know you from another one of the smelly humans in that place." As gross as it was, I rubbed the paint and grime off the Dramen's dead body and painted Emrys's pretty pale face with it. I thought the tough spider was going to vomit his guts, but he held it in. He was bound by blood to me, to help, and I appreciated his willingness to be here.

"Thank you all for coming, for being here with me." Dris, Desmire, Rune, and Emrys gave me hope in this bond. . . this little circle of friendship we had created.

"It is our honor." Dris curtsied in a fun mocking way and Emrys, who looked exactly like a Dramen, smiled excitedly. Desmire stood, ready to carry us to the place that looked like a nightmare brought to life, and Rune . . .

I turned to the werewolf and looked him in the eyes. "Thank you."

He had been calm, diving down into that well of rage inside him, that place where he had no fight about ripping a man's head off with his teeth.

"It's dark enough now. We can stay above the clouds and drop Emrys in. You guys ready to do this?"

The humming intensified beneath my skin, and my mind danced with the scent of revenge in the air. They nodding with resolve, not fear.

The city was a siren song of death, and we were ready for blood.

Chapter Fifty-Three

The city was lit only by torches. People fought in the streets randomly because they could. Decomposing heads of all colors and ages dripped blood down the spikes of the walls around the city. The castle was gray with iron everywhere. There were leafless vines growing up the side, adding to the eerie appearance. Laughter and screams were the soundtrack to this mission.

Rune growled from below. He hadn't wanted to sit on top of Desmire this time, so he stood on the dragon's hand with only his grip holding him to the dragon. He looked like a werewolf pirate staring at the city. The queen's balcony had been in the tallest part of the tower facing the east, so we swooped around with a quiet ease, and Emrys hopped off Desmire, rolling through his landing, then popped back up with an arrow nocked in the bow to shoot.

No one came after him, and after a few seconds, he lowered his bow and walked into the castle. My hands wouldn't stop fidgeting against the hem of the diamond armor, feeling it between my finger pads, testing it against my nails as we waited.

"Do you really think it will be this easy and he'll just pop back there with Tor?" Dris held onto me as we flew in circles high in the night's sky.

"No."

"Me, neither," she admitted, watching the balcony.

Five minutes went by, and Emrys hadn't come. People were still out in the roads of the city going about their own lives, so I believed everything was OK for now, and no one had caught onto us.

Suddenly, a loud noise echoed throughout the sky, and Rune roared just as Desmire turned to the left sharply. A fast flying ball of stone flew toward us. More shots and stones rained from the sky. They had seen us and knew we were here.

"Desmire, get us down!"

My grip struggled to keep up with his hairpin turns and speed. Dris was not faring well, either. Desmire's wings moved harder and faster as he swooped down toward the city. Fire sprayed from his mouth in a line, scorching everything below us.

"We need to jump," I told Dris, just as Desmire slowed by the queen's balcony again, and we leaped into the air, then landed with a hard cry. No one rushed to kill us or take our weapons, but it wouldn't be long. Desmire would cause havoc outside, and I didn't know if Rune was with him.

"We've got to move," I whispered to Dris, both of us standing as quietly as we could. The sounds of fire, and Desmire's roar drowned out the screams and shouts for blood from the Dramens both outside and inside the castle. With our weapons in hand, ready to fight, we took a step past the billowing curtains into the queen's room.

"She kinda has nice stuff," Dris commented, taking in the lavish furniture made of wood and gold and the large four-poster bed with chains wrapped around the top.

"I do not wanna know what those are for," Dris murmured and walked past the bed with haste.

Neither did I. The more we looked around the queen's room, the more disgusted I became. Weapons lined up in order on a dresser looked like a torture station, but there was no trace of blood anywhere.

It was obvious the King of the Dramens did not sleep in here. Despite the chains, the room oozed femininity with all the gold and luxury.

"Let's get out of here," I muttered. We managed to make it out of the queen's room and down the stairs before we ran into our first person, a normal-looking girl wearing a short dress and tie-up shoes. Her matted hair touched the pointed bones of her pelvis; her dirty body had splatters of blood over her tanned skin. There didn't appear to be any weapons on her, which I found odd.

"I don't know if we should kill her or save her," Dris whispered beside me as we stood there, weapons drawn. The woman watched us, not making a sound, but tilted her head from side to side like she couldn't figure out what she saw.

"Do you need help?" I asked, for some stupid reason. I asked despite that little warning in my head telling me to back away.

The woman's mouth opened wide, and she screamed. Her arms lifted with sharp fingernails and came straight for us. She was wild and would bite and claw until we were bloody scraps on the ground. Dris stepped in front of me. With her quick Fae movements, she smacked the girl's outstretched arms away, then hand chopped her three times against the side of the Dramen's neck. The girl went down instantly.

I stood there and thought my eyes were going to bulge out from my head. Dris turned to look at me with shaky hands, but then smiled.

"I'd read how to carotid chop from the *Elite Guards Manual*. Never thought I'd get to try it. I'll need to jot down in the notes that it did indeed make an attacker unconscious." Dris smiled.

Laughter bubbled up from my chest. Leave it to Dris to be a badass from reading books. We needed to move before the Dramen woke up. First we'd check the terrifying trophy room to see if Emrys was there.

We weaved through the halls, just like the survivor's encounter book said to do. Dris took the lead since she knew the layout better than I did. Her flawless memory was filled with the words of every book she'd read in her life.

"Oh, I'm going to puke." She gagged as we entered the room and saw heads and body parts of humans and beast hung on the red walls like trophies.

"Emrys." I covered my mouth and nose to keep the scents away.

"Emrys, if you're in here, get your ass out!" Dris yelled, her face ashen.

"I don't think he's here. We should head to the dungeon." I pulled Dris's arm toward the exit, not wanting to stay in this room any longer. Body, flesh, and organs hung like decorations. The Dramens were past redemption, past their humanity. They were evil.

Desmire had created a perfect distraction outside, so we made it to the holding cell with only going through two more unsuspecting Dramens. Dris used her chopping hands, and I managed to throw two hatchets into the chest of the other.

Emrys was picking the lock when we showed up. He was covered in unmentionable parts of humans and blood.

"You OK?" I asked my spider, relieved.

He nodded. "These are not humans; they are something else." Emrys's words were both a fact and a lie. They had been humans—were still technically human. They had changed into something brutal and bloodthirsty. I squeezed his shoulder.

"Prince Torin!" Dris gasped and I saw a man lying in a holding cell with five other people who looked at us with fear.

"Tor!" I breathed. Emotions flooded my chest. I sobbed, as I looked over his ripped clothes and dirty body on the stone floor.

"Sapphira?" He shook, his arms going around his torso like he held me instead of himself.

"I'm here, Tor, I'm here. This is real."

Emrys got the lock open, and I rushed in. The other's gaped, like they didn't know whether to run or fight me.

"You're free. They are distracted but not for long. Go!" They didn't need to be told again. Dris offered the biggest man her dagger and he accepted with only a nod.

"Tor." I called his name again, this time daring to touch him. He turned over slowly. His deep-blue eyes focused on me and softened, then he smiled.

"I was dreaming of you," he whispered, like he was still away in a dream of us.

Us.

With great effort, Tor stood. He took in my new appearance, and I knew he saw a new woman. I had packed on muscle. My skin wasn't as sunken in from lack of nutrition. My posture was that of a survivor, not the broken girl he had known. I was someone else entirely, changed in just these short weeks.

So much had changed.

He brought his lips to mine, only for the barest of seconds, though it felt like years. I pulled back and hugged him tightly, sadness and happiness mixing together in the pit of my stomach. Too much had changed, and I wasn't the same girl anymore.

Chapter Fifty-Four

"We've gotta get out of here. Can you run? Can you fight?" He'd already been through so much.

He nodded, his lips pursed together, and I could tell he wanted to say more, but it wasn't the time. I reached around my back and lifted the bow and quiver off me, handing it to him. He was a master with an arrow, and I was lucky enough to have taken this set from one of the Dramen's we'd downed on the way here. We walked toward the exit, and he watched only me, not even taking in our companions, whose glances darted back and forth between us.

I was more afraid of *that* conversation I'd have to have with him than I was facing the Dramens who appeared in the hallway just outside the holding room. A woman stood in the middle of them. Her brown eyes were decorated with black makeup, and harsh tattoos covered her cheeks. She was fit, and her leather clothes were bound together by string. She carried a sword on her hip and a gun in the other. She had a cunning and carnal expression. The black-spiked crown on her blood-coated, blond hair suggested we had met the Dramen's queen.

Emrys didn't hesitate. With Fae speed, he whipped out the only gun we had and fired. Tor nocked an arrow and shot two of the queen's guards.

"Run!" Dris screamed, and we took off down the hall, away from the shouting and very angry queen behind us. A howl echoed through the castle, and my body zinged at the sound. Rune was near and alive.

"He came?" Tor's surprised tone was not hidden through his heavy breaths. My body tensed from his words.

"This way." Emrys led us through the maze of halls toward an exit. A Dramen bellowed, coming from a room we hadn't looked in. The knife in his hand aimed for me. My hatchet crashed against his skull in seconds. I reacted without thinking. I pulled my blade from his head. Tor didn't know what to make of this new Sapphira. It bothered him, and I couldn't give him any reassurance now . . . maybe not ever.

The scent of smoke hit us as we leaped out into what looked like the courtyard. Fire ravaged the city. People didn't even try to fight the blaze torching their precious homes. The Dramens were firing cannons, which made loud booming noises. Gunshots were being fired toward the sky, and then close to us on the ground. A snarling roar echoed against the stone walls, and the sounds of screams came from inside the palace behind us.

"Desmire!" I shouted loudly, hoping the dragon heard my call.

Three Dramens came at us with weapons over their heads for a kill. Dris blocked one sword with hers, sweat dripping from her shimmering face as she gritted her teeth from the force of clashing steel. Tor engaged in battle with another, summoning enough strength to block, punch, and kick the Dramen's legs out from under him. His hand grasped an arrow and dug its pointed blade into the neck of the evil man. Emrys threw his only dagger into the chest of the other.

"Shit," he said. The hungry crowd of bloodthirsty Dramens wanting revenge came out of the smoke, right for us . . . with the king of the feral people at its center.

Chapter Fifty-Five

"Desmire! Rune!" I screamed, the panic in my voice was not forced or fake but terrifyingly real. We could not fight off this small army.

"We've got maybe thirty seconds until our blades clash with theirs." Dris shook with fear as she lifted her sword, preparing for battle.

My eyes met with Tor's. There was so much we needed to say, feelings to talk about, and answers to hear.

"You came for me," he said, trying to make me feel better . . . always trying to bring me out of the dark place in my head that threatened to crush me.

"I did." Now we would all die together. I raised my sword at the roaring creatures who wanted to feast on our blood.

A lifeless body was flung into view on our right, and the stones beneath my feet quivered as a large werewolf stepped in front of me. His sharp teeth and rippling roar stopped the Dramens. Blood dripped from Rune's claws, and I knew his teeth would be the same. Suddenly, a black mass dropped from the sky with large wings spread wide, crushing the stones beneath the weight.

Desmire attacked, shooting fire at the crowd. He swiped his large spiked tail toward the fleeing people who shot at him.

"Get on! Now!" I screamed, and my friends began to run.

Rune's snout lifted, baring teeth like he was about to growl at his brother but then stopped when I grabbed onto his hand and pulled him toward the dragon. We needed to leave before we lost our chance. Rune made sure everyone was loaded on Desmire first, before stepping onto the dragon's hand again. I smiled from the victory. We'd actually done it.

Out the corner of my eye, I saw the Dramen queen with a spear in her outstretched arms. Everything moved in slow motion as I watched the weapon leave the queen's hands. Desmire's vast wings began to rise, his feet lifted, a position ready to shoot us into the sky. The queen's face held a smile on her lips, as the spear flew straight and true toward my wildly beating heart.

"No!" Tor screamed; his hand reached out to stop the spear but the queen had made a calculated move. Desmire's body lifted, and I was going to be in the spear's path. A mass of black fur blocked my sight, almost knocking me off Desmire. A high-pitched howl ripped my world into shreds as a metal blade protruded through the gut of the werewolf hovering over me. Rune's eyes closed, and his mouth went slack.

"Grab him!" Tor said, and Dris and Emrys shot into action. Rune was falling, the spear in his gut going with him, and no one was quick enough to grab him.

"Desmire, please!" I pleaded though my sobs. The dragon dove and clutched the cursed prince in his claws, before lifting us up into the night sky.

My heart couldn't take anymore. I was tired of losing those I loved, tired of seeing people in unnecessary pain and anguish. I was tired of fighting. I let myself fall into a deep sleep that wrapped around me.

"Sleep, Sapphira. I'll make sure you are safe," Tor whispered in my ear, and I managed to nod.

As I shut down every agonizing thought, I went far into my mind, a place where things that had been locked away for too long broke free of their forgotten prison.

"I'm sorry we didn't have more time." I looked at my father, who looked like me with the same light brown skin and wild brown hair. His smoky gray eyes were brought to life with the smile on his face. Little laugh lines creased above his cheeks. He was tall and broad unlike the man who had raised me. He was the warrior my mother always loved . . . her mate. She had drawn the tattoos on his face in a moment of peace between them.

I wanted to believe Rune and I would have ended up better than them. Better than this. She had gone on to marry Verin to protect our lands and sired me with Desmire. I'd read it in her journal, then she told me of their story, and I felt my heart expand for them. He was the father I never got to experience.

Verin was cold and never once held me or tucked me in as I grew.

"We will. This is not our end. And when you return my daughter, we will fight together."

I managed to hold back my tears. My mother touched my shoulder, and I knew our final moment had come.

"I will come back for you," I promised her. "You will be a great queen . . . loved and fiercer than I ever could have been. The warrior spirit in you cannot be broken. You will fight, and there will be nothing that can stop you." She pulled me in for a hug. Her shoulders shook with emotion in my embrace. My father wrapped his arms around us, and despite what was to come, I knew all would be OK.

"Mariam will keep you safe from now on. Trust your gut no matter what, and don't cause too much trouble." My mother released her grasp around me and stood at the altar where my handmaiden Nyx waited in her purple dress for her final task.

The darkness was coming, and this was the only way.

With my hands clasped in my parents, we released our magic one last time.

Chapter Fifty-Six

I woke with a lump in my throat and tears on my cheeks.

"Shh. Sapphira. You're safe. You're home."

Dris.

I opened my eyes. I wasn't on Desmire or on the ground in the forest somewhere, but in Crysia. Light shined in through pale blue curtains, giving the room a soft brightness.

"We made it," I whispered. The words didn't seem real. "Where am I?" I sat up, and a blanket fell off my chest.

"The queen's room. Tor is talking with her outside the door with Emrys. Rune is in the healer's quarters. And well . . ." She smiled. "Desmire sort of crash-landed into the onyx room. We were lucky that no one got impaled on those dreadful crystal spikes." She shook her head at the image. "Verin is gone, by the way. Supposedly the king . . ." she wrinkled her nose at the word "king" ". . . has gone away on important business. No one knows when he will return."

The news was not surprising. He had the truth of my identity now and would hide in his castle while he devised an evil plan, which would bring agony to this world and my life. But that all would have to wait for another day. On shaky muscles, I rose to my feet.

"Are you sure you wanna do this?" Dris understood what I had to do and didn't need her aunt's gifts to confirm it.

"I just want to get it over with. The past weeks have been focused on saving Tor and getting Nyx out of that damn tomb. My life is about to follow a hard path that will either destroy me to my core or create something unimaginable. I just need to do it, move on, and control what I can. No more hiding."

She nodded and reached her hand out for mine. My friend. Together we walked out of the room.

The queen looked at me with the same spirit burning in her eyes from the queen of the vision I'd had. She knew me. She'd known all along, just like Tor, like Celestine.

"Sapphira." Tor rushed to me. His hand touched my face softly, the relief in him visible as he shuddered from his touch on my skin.

"Tor, I need to ask you a question. No more hiding and no more lies."

I know he hadn't done it out of malicious intent, but he had kept the truth from me before. His hands moved down from my cheeks to my shoulders. "No lies," he promised.

"What was the princess's power?"

Tor smiled sadly, for he knew everything was about to change as soon as I opened the onyx tomb and freed Nyx. Our worlds were going to be flipped upside down. This was the endgame all along. It was why Tor was sent to get me, to bring me here, and go through all the training, confusion, visions, and rescue.

I had to go through it all to find out the truth and feel it in my very soul.

"Absorption. She could touch another Fae and take some of their powers. Once inside her body, she always had a part of them."

And just like that, I knew what I had to do. I focused on one thing, and the rest would fall into place.

"I need to see Rune," I said and walked toward the healer's quarters. Tor, the queen, and my friends followed. We made it as far as the throne room before the sound of an angry woman echoed in the hallways.

Rune appeared, his body leaning against the wall for balance. He was back in normal Fae form and looked tired as hell. The healer chased him and scolded him about moving. Rune ignored her, like he did everyone else and staggered to me. He winced with every step, gritting his teeth through the pain, and teetered his way to a few feet in front of me. His attention shifted to his brother who stood behind me, and his jaw hardened.

He still didn't know. Although his heart and wolf did, the man still couldn't see the truth in front of him.

"Moon is here." The queen smiled while looking at the diamond tree still missing some leaves from the fray with Verin's men.

Those were three of the first words she had said when I arrived at the palace. It made sense now. So many things I should have seen or heard. If I had just been open to them, I could have pieced together the clues. Tor had never slept with me because he knew who I was. The queen did not try and drown me to get me out of Verin's sight—she wanted me to get to the cave behind the waterfall but couldn't tell me. She didn't know she was hurting me. She knew I'd be OK if I could just hide from her evil husband.

"I need the necklace the princess gave you." I held out my hand toward him. Reluctantly, his trembling hand reached up to untie the necklace from his battered neck.

"Thank you for keeping it safe." I walked into the onyx room and saw Desmire curled up beside the tomb, sleeping like a cat with his tail under his snout.

"Desmire."

The dragon's lids flew open. His stare shifted from each of my companions behind me to the queen and finally settled on me.

"I need your strength." I held the necklace out for him to see the onyx circle in my hand. It was his onyx but not made by his core. His powers had been taken and used to hide something invaluable.

I'd solved the puzzle and it was time to see the final picture. All of us needed to see it. Desmire opened his snout, and I walked over to put the little circle between his teeth. "All I need is a crack. Don't shatter it, please." I stepped back.

Slowly the dragon's jaw began to close, the onyx trembled between two sharp teeth. We heard a "crack" and the necklace fell toward the ground. I was able to grab it before it broke into tiny pieces on the tile floor.

The final piece of the puzzle. So tiny it could have been mistaken for a piece of sand. In the onyx lay the key.

Chapter Fifty-Seven

"What is it?" Dris asked from behind me, the little dark dot in my hand with the broken onyx in the other.

"It's the key to getting her out of there." Nyx's sacrifice was over.

"How is that the key?" Emrys asked curiously.

"It has magic in it, magic that was encased in onyx to protect it from the curse, which is the main essence of onyx."

"Core magic only works with the Fae who holds that particular core." Rune looked more confused than any of them. He was going to hate me, but I couldn't take it back and change what had been done.

"Right," I confirmed, before my eyes closed and the familiar essence sang a song that only I understood. The tiny dark blue gem, hidden in the onyx for safekeeping, held just enough power to open the onyx tomb.

Gasps echoed around the room, and I knew that what I'd read in Gregory Debaru's experiment book worked. I absorbed my essence back and became a little closer to being whole again.

Fae.

The word held new meaning as the yearning in my soul mingled with the essence of the gem I'd absorbed back into my body. I touched the onyx, and it began to melt around Nyx, exposing her to the air for the first time in twenty years. With the exposure came the memories that had been trapped inside of everyone who had been affected. It had been the queen's plan to help hide what had been done from Verin. The queen had lost her power because she had used it all to wipe her daughter out of the minds of everyone and replace the image with the woman still laying on the altar. Now they remembered it was me all along; she was just the decoy.

"My moon," Rune breathed, as he stared at me. A sob rose from my chest. I wanted to dart to his side, to see his face, but I wasn't done and I knew there would be no resisting the pull once I fell prey to it.

I moved the onyx behind the tomb and touched the pale skin of Nyx's fingers.

The sleeping woman began to wake up, her eyes blinked over and over as she adjusted to the light and scents around her.

"You did it." She spoke hoarsely. I smiled at the purple-haired woman peering at me as tears rolled down her cheeks.

"You did it." My hand wrapped around hers, thanking her, my old handmaiden, for what she had done for me, what she had given up. She had layed in that onyx for twenty years until I was ready and could return to finally take on the darkness. She was willing to let everyone believe she was me.

"Here." She lifted her shaky hands and removed the necklace with the large dark-blue stone from her body. The precious gem's vibrations called me, wanting to come home.

"That's not what I think it is, is it?" Emrys asked.

I chuckled. "It's my core. I'd hidden it in the onyx with the help of my parents, and then with Nyx to preserve the essence and magic until I could come back and retrieve it."

Every step I made was like turning in mud. It was hard to face those behind me.

"I had forgotten who I was. The process of taking out my essence had given me amnesia. I remember who I am now. I am Princess Sapphira of Crysia, daughter of Desmire and Queen Olyndria. And this is my sapphire core." I pressed the hard stone to my chest and closed my eyes. Power tingled in my chest, like the feeling of nerves firing in a limb that had long been numb. I was becoming whole and new but yet the familiar sensation of coming home wrapped around me.

Without the core, I hadn't died . . . I had become a human. I followed every step Gregory Debaru had done in his book and it actually worked. I had taken my core out of my body to keep it safe and hide it in plain sight. The power of all I had touched and absorbed before flared in my chest, making me wobble from the onslaught of magic I'd long forgotten how to hold in my body.

"Princess." Tor's voice was laced with awe. Tears glistened on the queen's cheeks, knowing her daughter had become whole once again. Dris patted Emrys on the back since he was in shock. My focal point shifted from his perfect face to that of my mate.

My mate.

My mate.

I had turned from the truth out of guilt and fear. The yearning I'd dreamed of was here, alive, and burning in my soul so brightly like the moon had hidden its light inside me. He sensed it, too. The trembling in his hands had nothing to do with the lack of strength but the need to reach out to me, to feel me underneath his touch. *Soon.*

My ears grew into points, and my skin glowed with the shimmer of a gem weaved in my blood. Transforming into Fae once more, random memories I'd forgotten returned, and I changed into a new me, from Fae princess to human survivor of the apocalypse and back. I'd gone on a hero's journey and became a stronger, better version of myself. The warrior who stood for those who couldn't, who fought for what I believed in, and who would bring a greater world for the Fae and humans.

And I would start by bringing magic back.

The End... For now

Sapphira's Story Continues in

A Truth In Ruby

Now Available

Link- mybook.to/ATruthInRuby

Add to your Goodreads TBR- https://bit.ly/39RqH2O

More Books by Jessica Florence

https://www.jessicaflorenceauthor.com/books

Dawn (Hero Society #1)

Dawn has come, a time for heroes to rise. Draco has lived long and felt the pain of loss more than anyone in one lifetime could imagine.

Immortality was given to him as a gift, a gift that failed him and turned him into a shell of the man that has nothing left but to wait out the end of existence alone.

Until her.

Rose is an empath who sees more than who Draco is supposed to be: she sees him, and what they could be. Together, they will begin the search for others with extraordinary powers, to stop a war that's been brewing for over a millennia.

The journey is only beginning, and an unnamed enemy has started to make his mark on their world.

The dawn of heroes has finally arrived.

Only time will tell if it's too late to defeat the upcoming darkness of night that now descends upon all of mankind.

The Final KO

I fight for a living.

Which makes finding a decent guy hard when you're a female MMA fighter. None of them have been my equal. I yearn for a man who can push me to reach new heights and challenge me. A man who will treat me like a lady then lift me up by my ass and impale me against the wall.

But when Arson Kade, MMA's top fighter and notorious manwhore, declares he's that man for me I have my doubts. Any sane woman would.

There seems to be more to Arson than the rumors that surround him, but will it make me fall hard or run for the hills?
I know I've got no choice but to hold on for the ride.

It's the main event and my heart's on the line.
But will it be the Final KO?

The Final Chase

I never thought one day I'd make a bet about pedicures to a man and loose.

But of course, I'd never man like him.
Jake Wild. Owner of Wild rescue for exotic animals.
He's everything I'm not, my polar opposite.
I'm heels and my salon,
He's dirt and his creatures.
But much like the animals he cares for, he's got that carnal edge.
He's the type of man you crawl on your hands and knees for.
He bites, he's on the hunt, and now I'm his prey
A chance meeting and a bet started the undeniable attraction between us.
But I'm not giving my heart and soul away that easy, he's going to have to catch me first.
It's the ultimate game of cat and mouse,
But will it be our Final Chase?

Long Drive

There is a long road in everyone's journey in life.
For some people, it's a way to get from one place to another.
For others, it's a search for one's purpose in existence.
For me, the road was where I could find peace.
When everything in my life had shattered, I turned to the road.
And that's where I met him.
Killian Lemarque.
A beautiful truck driver, and my salvation.
One month on the road together is the deal, and when it's over, I will have hopefully figured out what I'm going to do about my torn reality.
But sometimes the road can change everything. Falling in love wasn't part of my plan nor his.

But here we are.
One Month. One Truck. One Long Drive.

How You Get The Girl

As Hollywood's hottest actor, getting a woman in my bed is never a challenge.

But after seeing a feisty woman in bar who was looking for a one-night stand, I knew that her being in my bed wouldn't be enough.

She turned me down, and I thought I'd never see her again.

Fate had other plans though.

Alessandra Rose is now my lead makeup artist for the next four months. Literally, her job is to touch me every day for the duration of filming. Sounds like a win, right?

Nope, she stops me at every hint of a flirt. I'm in uncharted waters for once.

Her argument is good I'll give her that. I'm a good actor, so accepting that it's not all an act would be tough.

But I'm not going anywhere; here heart is my Grammy and him here to win it.

 That's how you get the girl.

INSPIRED

Call it pure desperation, or maybe we'd agree it was the lack of sleep that had me signing six weeks of my life away to be bossed around by a life coach. Either way, I was trying to get my life together, and Logan Woodland was going to help.

I thought he'd make me eat healthier, drink more water, and do yoga. What I wasn't expecting, was to be forced to see myself as I was and how far I'd fallen.

But then his program worked.

He'd shown me a life filled with passion and desire. A life where I was stronger and could be the woman I'd never known existed inside me.

I did have a six-week life-changing experience, but now, I wanted more than I'd signed on for.

Him.

Guiding Lights

He sings of suffering. His eyes hold the pain of living in sorrow.
The moment our gaze meets recognition flares within.
We are tortured souls drifting in a sea of darkness.
He knows I have secrets that I'll never tell.
I am numb.
I am broken.
I can never be the guiding light through the darkness he thinks I am.
I have forsaken my past, I rely on keeping myself shut off.
I wish things were different, that maybe we could be each other's lifeline.
But destiny drags us down like an anchor.
He lives his life in the lime light of a famous rock star, and I live in shadows on the run.

I wished I'd known that before I fell for him, but now it's too late.

Blinding Lights

She dances with a passion I'll never know.
Seeing her again tears me at the seams.
She was never mine.
My soul is stained with the darkness of death.
I have killed.
I have tortured.
I have lost.
Her soul is too bright for the shadows I live in
and her determination to be the flame in my heart
could kill us both.
Still, I want her, I crave her.
But not even her blinding lights can fight away the
darkness threatening us both.

But I refuse to lose her, and this time I don't think I can
walk away.

Weighing of the Heart

What happens when the myths of old become reality?

Thalia Alexander has lived her life in peace until her twenty-fifth birthday when she has a strange dream about a man.

A tall, dark, and sexy man that shows up at her work the next morning.

Tristan Jacks is trouble with a capital T, but for some strange reason she is drawn to him like nothing she has ever experienced before. He has this possessiveness and adoration for her that she can't explain. It's like they have known each other forever.

Thalia's strange dreams continue to stalk her as her relationship with Tristan builds to be a love that will last the ages.

And when those dreams and reality start to clash, will Thalia be able to handle the truth?

Could the world of ancient myths truly exist in modern times?

Evergreen

It was supposed to be an easy stakeout.
Until a bunch of bachelorettes mobbed me, changing my life forever.

I couldn't get Andi Slaton, with her red hair, blue eyes, and cotton candy-flavored lip gloss, out of my head.

But when she offers herself to aid the FBI to help me take down the biggest criminal family in Tampa, Florida, my very sanity is put to the test watching her spend time with my arch enemy.

She's everything I want, I will be everything to her.
We will be Evergreen.

Acknowledgments

I know I dedicated this book to them, but I have to give another round of thanks to Karen, who took the blinders off my eyes, to Lorriane, who has helped me grow into a better author than I imagined, to Becca for ASIO's cover, to Rochelle and her gift of stock photos, and to Casey who gave me a shot with help from her PR people.

I would not have been able to pull off releasing this book when I did had it not been for these ladies. Just when I thought life as I knew it was ending, it was really a new beginning.

Thank you to every single person who has ever given me a chance. I love you and will forever be grateful for the opportunity.

Thank you to my friends, my family, my fellow authors. You guys give me strength when I run low.

Cassie, Lorriane, Virginia. I appreciate your work so much. You've helped me create the best product I could ever put out. I am so happy to have found you all.

To my Fairies, you are everything and I love you.

To my JFlo Promo Society, and my promo supporters, I wouldn't be here without you.

To anyone who has a dream, I am here for you. You can reach them, and I hate to sound cliché but all you have to do is believe it before you see it. Don't let anyone tell you differently.

Thank you. Thank you. Thank you.

I'm so honored to have this opportunity to earn a place on your bookshelf.

Finally,

Thank you to my husband, who supports me and my passions no matter what. I love you babe and I am sooo freaking happy I have you.

To my Peanut Butter girl, Thank you for letting me be your mommy, and inspiring me every day.

About the Author

Jessica Florence writes the stories that her fellow nerds yearn for.

From Superheroes to Sexy Truckers, Jessica is known to give readers unique tales of hope where love conquers all. Stories that melt away reality and take you on a journey with the characters. If escapism is what you are looking for, then look no further. Jessica is the Queen of weaving the tales you may not normally pick up but find yourself not being able to put down.

Jessica's always had a love of reading, and her love of books lead her to start writing in the 9th grade. She quickly learned that storytelling was her passion. Inspired by movies, music, and her personal life she writes like it's the very air she breathes. Through her writing it's evident that she lives for the stories she creates.

Jessica grew up in North Carolina, and currently resides in Southwest Florida with her daughter, husband, and German Shepherd. She loves to be outside, write in her hammock, and collect tea mugs.

CONNECT WITH J-FLO:

→ FACEBOOK: facebook.com/jessicaflorenceauthor
→ INSTAGRAM: Instagram.com/authorjessicaflorence
→ TWITTER: twitter.com/@Florence_jess

→ PINTEREST: pinterest.com/florencejess
→ WEBSITE: www.Jessicaflorenceauthor.com

Printed in Great Britain
by Amazon